DEFIANT LOVE

DEFIANT LOVE

Joanne Lennox

Chivers Press • Thorndike Press
Bath, England • Waterville, Maine USA

This Large Print edition is published by Chivers Press, England, and by Thorndike Press, USA.

Published in 2002 in the U.K. by arrangement with the author.

Published in 2002 in the U.S. by arrangement with Dorian Literary Agency.

U.K. Hardcover ISBN 0–7540–4831–4 (Chivers Large Print)
U.S. Softcover   ISBN 0–7862–3943–3 (Nightingale Series Edition)

23 **FICTION**

The text of this Large Print edition is unabridged.
Other aspects of the book may vary from the original edition.

Set in 16 pt. New Times Roman.

Printed in Great Britain on acid-free paper.

British Library Cataloguing in Publication Data available

Library of Congress Cataloging-in-Publication Data

Lennox, Joanne.
    Defiant love / by Joanne Lennox.
        p.   cm.
    ISBN 0–7862–3943–3 (lg. print : sc : alk. paper)
    1. Large type books. I. Title.
    PR6062.E647 D44 2002
    823'.92—dc21   2001058469

CHAPTER ONE

Standing on tiptoes, her right arm outstretched, Sophie glanced round when she heard a voice unknown to her. The man who had spoken was tall with dark, curling brown hair, casually but neatly dressed in black denims and a crisp white T-shirt.

'Can I help you?' the stranger repeated.

From the sound of his voice, he wasn't from round these parts.

'It's all right,' Sophie replied, politely but firmly.

All her life she had been used to people assuming that because of her diminutive build and stature, she was incapable of looking after herself.

'I can manage, thank you!'

But the man had reached out towards the jar of grapefruit marmalade on the top shelf without waiting for her reply. As they both tussled over the jar, it toppled off the shelf and crashed to the floor. For a moment the two of them just stared at it in dismay.

'Look what you've done now,' the man said irritatedly.

'Me?' Sophie's eyes widened. 'I'd have been perfectly all right if it hadn't been for you interfering!'

They glared at each other, neither willing to back down. Then the man bent to pick up a large, jagged piece of glass, just as a middle-aged woman in supermarket uniform appeared.

'Does anything seem to be the matter?'

She stopped short, noticing the shattered jar on the floor.

'Oh, dear!'

'I was just helping this young lady to clear up the mess,' the man explained with a belittling glance at Sophie.

'You were helping me?' Sophie didn't believe her ears. 'That's rich, considering it was you who caused the accident in the first place!'

'Perhaps,' he remarked drily, 'you should stop arguing and help clear up this mess.'

'I haven't got time to spare cleaning up someone else's mess!' Sophie said exasperatedly.

She had more important things on her mind, like the phone call she had received that morning.

The shop assistant returned with a dustpan and brush.

'I'll pay for the breakage, of course,' Sophie offered.

'No, I'll pay for the breakage.' The man sighed exaggeratedly. 'As you seem to hold me responsible, I suppose it's the least I can do.'

There was something attractively rugged about him, Sophie thought suddenly as she gazed at the man. He looked about as bleak as

2

a rock face, too, as if he rarely gave vent to emotions.

'It's all right,' a smooth voice behind them said, cutting into her thoughts. 'There's no charge for the breakage.'

The supermarket manager had materialised behind them. Chris Atkins, who was only a few years older than Sophie, also happened to be a friend of Sophie's father, both men being members of the local Rotary.

'Hello, Chris,' Sophie muttered.

'Is this man annoying you, Sophie?' Chris asked solicitously.

'No, it's all right thank you, Chris,' she answered reluctantly.

'I was just leaving anyway,' the man muttered, turning away. 'I've got everything I came in for.'

Sophie had, too. Unfortunately, the two of them chose the same moment to push their trolleys off down the narrow aisle, and they barged into each other with an ominous clash of metal.

'Hey, watch it!' Sophie exclaimed.

The man stood back impatiently for her to pass.

'After you!' he barked, sounding anything but chivalrous.

'No, after you.'

Stubbornly, Sophie dug her heels in, but the man was equally stubborn in his refusal to budge. If one of them didn't back down soon, they could be there all night. Sighing, Sophie gave in, pushing her trolley off down the aisle to the checkout.

There was only one checkout open and she joined the queue. Just at that moment, however, another was opened and the dark-haired stranger promptly pushed his trolley straight through. For Sophie it was the final straw.

'Queue jumper!' she seethed under her breath.

The man gazed impertinently round at her as if he had heard what she had said. To her fury, Sophie found herself looking away, intimidated by that dark glare.

Within minutes, the man's shopping had been packed and paid for and he stalked out of the shop without a backward glance. Sophie leaned against her trolley, sighing in relief.

*   *   *

'Good evening, everyone.'

Jean Chapman, chairperson and host of that night's meeting, smiled around the gleaming dining-room table.

'First of all this evening, I'd like to introduce Ecclesdon Crafts' newest recruit, James Harrison. James is a woodturner.'

Sophie's first thought was that there was something strangely familiar about James Harrison. Her eyes fixed on the man who sat

4

to the left of Jean's position at the head of the table. Now, where had she seen him before? Suddenly it struck her. He was the man from the supermarket!

Jean was working her way round the table making the introductions to the co-workers of the little craft shop. They were an unlikely collection of people, brought together simply by circumstance and their common creative skills. On Jean's right sat old Tom Bradley, a renowned local oil-painter, then next to him was middle-aged divorcée, Mary Howard, a potter. Then there was Sophie's friend, Mandy Benson, who arranged flowers, and finally large, capable Jean herself, who made silk waistcoats.

'And this is Sophie Taylor,' Jean said suddenly, jolting Sophie out of her reveries. 'Sophie paints watercolours,' she added, by way of explanation.

'Pleased to meet you,' Sophie mumbled, steeling herself to meet his gaze.

'I believe we've already met,' James Harrison replied, looking directly at her for the first time.

So he had remembered. Sophie blushed. His eyes were so dark that she was unable to read their expression. It could be anything from mocking to amused.

'Now, James, have you got any questions about the running of the shop?' Jean was asking.

This was a big mistake, as Sophie all too soon realised. James Harrison apparently had several questions, which he ran through with the quiet precision of a general planning a military operation. She soon got the impression that he was a man who liked things done tidily and properly.

'How is space allocated within the shop?' he queried. 'My woodwork takes up a considerable amount of room.'

'Space is shared equally. I'm sure you will have plenty of room,' Jean told him diplomatically. 'Of course we'll be happy to listen to any suggestions you may have once you've had a look round.'

Sophie sighed, glancing surreptitiously at her watch while another question was asked and answered. Did they have to waste time on these tiresome minor details, when there was much more important business to attend to?

'And what are the security arrangements at the shop? Some of my pieces are worth hundreds of pounds.'

'This is supposed to be a friendly, little co-operative,' Sophie pointed out, unable to keep quiet any longer, 'not a multi-million pound conglomerate!'

'I'm sure you'll find the security arrangements at the shop perfectly adequate,' Jean continued as if Sophie had not spoken.

Sophie lapsed into silence, doodling on her copy of the agenda while the newcomer continued with his questioning. At last, when he had filed away the appropriate answers, he leaned back in his chair, his face settling once again into a frown.

'Now for the evening's other business,' Jean said briskly.

She handed everyone a copy of the work rota for the coming month, then went on to discuss the arrangements for Ecclesdon's annual craft show, which was due to take place in just over a fortnight's time. But Sophie's eyes remained firmly fixed on the final item on the agenda, for any other business.

The previous day, she had received a phone call from Steve Collins, a friend from her college days and nowadays a member of a conservation group and a keen environmental activist.

'Sophie, bad news I'm afraid,' he had greeted her dramatically. 'It looks like our last-ditch efforts have been in vain. The council has voted that work on the new supermarket can go ahead. The building contractors have been given permission to begin clearing the heath next week.'

Sophie's reaction had been one of dismay. Ecclesdon, a small Dorset town set in beautiful scenery and whose economy relied heavily on tourism, had so far managed to remain virtually unscathed by modern developments. For some months, she had supported Steve wholeheartedly in his campaign to stop the council from allowing a supermarket to be built on Ecclesdon Heath, an area of land to the north of the town. It was a haven for wildlife and there was a long-standing, local campaign for it to be made a site of Special Scientific Interest.

'Don't worry,' Steve had assured her. 'We're not giving up yet. We're calling an emergency meeting at the town hall on Friday. Be there if you can, and tell everyone you know.'

'Does anybody have any other business?' Jean asked, bringing Sophie's thoughts back to the present.

Sophie raised her hand, eagerly seizing her chance.

'I expect most of you have heard about the proposals to build a supermarket on Ecclesdon Heath,' she began, 'and the campaign to stop them from going ahead.'

Murmurs and nods from around the table encouraged her to go on.

'As you know, these proposals pose a serious threat to our environment. Not only will it be threatened if they go ahead, but local businesses will suffer a crippling loss of trade.'

Again there were murmurs of agreement.

'They're calling a public meeting at the town hall on Friday,' Sophie continued. 'Anyone who's interested is invited to attend. They're hoping to bring in council officers to answer questions. This could be our final chance to make ourselves heard!'

8

'Of course we'll all be there!' Mandy assured her.

'They should be protecting that land, not destroying it!' Mary Howard added feelingly.

Only the new man, James Harrison, remained silent. Determined to let bygones be bygones, Sophie turned to him with a friendly smile.

'What about you, James? Can we count on your support?'

His dark eyes held hers for a moment before he answered.

'Actually,' he said, 'I think there are several good reasons why the building of the supermarket should go ahead.'

Deathly silence greeted his words. For a moment Sophie was speechless. She hadn't expected to be challenged, not over something as serious as this.

'Such as?' she asked indignantly, when her voice had returned to her.

'What about the lower prices the supermarket will guarantee for local people, and the jobs that will be created?' James Harrison suggested. 'Not to mention the extra families and businesses that will be attracted to the area?'

'But do we really want Ecclesdon to become overrun with tourists?' Sophie countered.

James Harrison shrugged, undeterred.

'All I'm saying is that perhaps Ecclesdon should move with the times.'

'And what gives you the right to say that?'

'What do you mean?' he asked in surprise.

'You seem to think you know better than people who have lived here all their lives.'

Sophie tucked a stray strand of hair behind her ear, her eyes alight now.

'Sophie,' their chairwoman interrupted tactfully, 'go easy on the poor man!'

But James Harrison was clearly more than capable of sticking up for himself.

'You're right,' he said to Sophie. 'I have just moved down to Dorset, from Croydon, as a matter of fact. But as anyone who has always lived in an urban area will tell you, the countryside is special. I may not be a native, but I care about this area as much as you do,'

Sophie had to admit she was surprised by the emotion behind his words, but she covered it by retorting, 'Well, you've got a funny way of showing it!'

The rest of the group had fallen silent, and sat content to watch the two of them fighting it out amongst themselves.

'That's the trouble with environmental issues,' James Harrison replied coolly. 'They're too emotive, and people can often be blind to the actual facts of the matter.'

Fat chance of this man getting emotive about anything, Sophie fumed silently, glaring at him. She was infuriated by his cool self-assurance, but even more so by her suspicions that in a way he was right. If she had

10

researched her facts a little better, she might have been more of a match for him.

She wished suddenly that Steve Collins was there. He always had the relevant facts and figures at his fingertips. She was sure that Steve would have a suitable response to every one of James Harrison's well thought-out arguments!

'I take it you won't be coming to the meeting on Friday, then?' Sophie said sarcastically.

'I haven't decided yet.'

Sophie nodded, her mouth twisting knowingly. She knew that meant he would not attend.

James Harrison withdrew back into himself after their heated exchange, and shortly afterwards, the meeting broke up. People drifted out of Jean's house, calls of thanks and farewell echoing on the mild night air. Sophie hovered by the door, waiting for Mandy Benson to fetch her jacket. The two women lived a couple of streets away from each other and usually walked part of the way home together.

Suddenly the tall figure of James Harrison was standing in front of her, dwarfing her.

'Can I give you a lift?' he asked curtly, his car keys dangling from one long-fingered hand.

For a moment Sophie was taken aback by the offer. She would have expected James

Harrison to give her a wide berth after the tongue-lashing she had given him earlier.

'No thank you,' she said, covering her surprise, adding haughtily, 'The fresh air will do me good!'

'Are you sure you'll be safe, a lone woman walking the streets at night?'

James Harrison's brows knit into their habitual frown. Instinctively Sophie bristled, resenting this slur on her independence.

'I don't believe in using the car for short journeys,' she retorted.

She wasn't usually this argumentative, but there was something about the man that really got her goat!

'Why pollute the atmosphere unnecessarily, when you could just as easily walk?'

James Harrison was about to reply when Mandy appeared behind them.

'Did I hear someone mention a lift?' she asked. 'How kind of you, James. Sophie and I would be delighted to accept.'

'Speak for yourself, Mandy. I'm quite happy to walk!'

Sophie glared furiously at her friend.

'As James has been kind enough to offer us a lift,' Mandy replied airily, 'the least we can do is accept graciously.'

She flashed Sophie a look that dared her to defy her. Sophie stared speechlessly back at her friend. What was Mandy up to now? To her surprise and, she had to admit, her annoyance, it looked as though she was flirting with their new member. Well, it was hardly anything to do with her if her misguided friend wanted to make advances towards the aloof, arrogant James Harrison.

Aged twenty-six, a year older than Sophie, Mandy had already been through one unsuccessful marriage, not to mention a string of short-lived romances. Sophie had first met Mandy when she herself was not long out of art college, trying without success to find a job in a firm of graphic designers.

Most of her college friends had left to find jobs in London, but Sophie was reluctant to leave the sparkling seas and rolling green hills of Dorset, although, as her well-meaning parents had pointed out to her, she was throwing away the chance of a good career.

By chance, Sophie had spotted an advert in a local newspaper giving details of a vacancy at the local craft shop, The position would involve working part-time at the shop and contributing a share of the rent of the premises. Until then, Sophie's watercolours had been purely an enjoyable hobby, but, paying a visit more out of curiosity than anything else, she had been pleasantly surprised by the small, efficiently-run shop with its tasteful displays.

Going to the desk to enquire further, she had met Mandy, working on a dried flower arrangement that was as neat and pretty as

Mandy was herself. Once Sophie had been accepted for the vacancy she and Mandy had become firm friends, Mandy filling the void left by the departure of Sophie's college friends.

The two young women were very different, especially when it came to relationships! Mandy threw herself into each new love affair with abandon, while Sophie was the opposite, stubbornly content with her own company, despite Mandy's frequent attempts to set up double dates for them.

'Come on, Sophie, aren't you coming?' Mandy was speaking insistently to her now.

'I suppose so.'

Conceding that she had no choice, Sophie gave a heavy sigh, reluctantly following the other two off down the garden path. A few minutes later she was clambering through to the back of James Harrison's old Morris estate car, which smelled enticingly of bees-wax polish and wood-shavings. Meanwhile Mandy settled herself in the front.

'So,' Mandy was saying brightly, 'what did you do for a living, when you lived in Croydon?'

Because of her willowy figure and pretty face, men usually assumed Sophie's friend to be a dumb blonde, which couldn't have been further from the truth. Once Mandy had set her sights on a man, most were powerless to resist her.

14

'What? Oh, I worked at a joiner's.'

'So why did you leave?' Mandy persisted.

'Decided I'd had enough, so I handed in my notice,' James Harrison replied economically, clearly not in the mood for polite conversation.

But Mandy was undaunted, and kept up a steady barrage of questions. Aware that her friend was up to her old tricks, Sophie smiled to herself, allowing her mind to drift away gently. She must have dozed off momentarily because the next thing she knew they were dropping Mandy off.

'You'll probably find it slightly more comfortable in the front,' James Harrison was saying to her, in such a tone that it was more of an order than a suggestion.

Sophie opened her mouth to argue. She was tired, and besides, she felt quite comfortable where she was. But something in the man's voice compelled her to obey.

'Do you often walk the streets on your own?' he asked gruffly when she had slid into the seat beside him.

At close quarters, Sophie was reminded once again of how attractive a man he was.

'What sort of a question's that?' she retorted, bending to clip on her seat-belt.

He ignored her comment, revving up the car and driving off.

'Don't you watch the news? Surely you realise the world's a dangerous place these days.'

'Not Ecclesdon,' Sophie replied loyally. 'Ecclesdon's safe.'

'Sadly, nowhere's safe these days, not even Ecclesdon,' he added.

Ironically, Sophie thought she would feel safer on the streets than in this car, with this worryingly attractive man only inches away from her, the smell of aftershave and woodshavings lingering headily on her nose.

'I prefer to be independent,' she said coolly, covering her discomfort, 'rather than a prisoner in my own home.'

'You don't own a car?'

'Yes, I do, actually,' Sophie replied, glancing at him. 'But, as I said—'

'You prefer not to use it for short journeys,' he finished for her, a hint of humour in his voice. 'Well,' he went on grimly, 'perhaps you ought to think less about saving the planet, and more about self-preservation.'

Sophie was silent. Despite the reproving nature of his tone, there was a concern in his voice that made her flush. Now that they were alone together she felt embarrassed about the way she had spoken to him earlier that evening. If they were to be work colleagues, they would have to set aside their personal differences and make an effort to get on with each other.

'I'm afraid I might have seemed a bit rude earlier,' she told him, forcing the words out.

'What's this? An apology?'

16

James Harrison frowned, not taking his eyes off the road as Sophie nodded.

'I shouldn't have said what I did. After all, you're new to the area, and I hardly laid down the welcome mat for you.'

He shook his head.

'I was equally to blame. I shouldn't have answered you back like that.'

Sophie frowned. He certainly didn't make it easy for her to apologise.

'It was my fault. I always talk first, think later.'

'I can't blame you for speaking out,' he replied. 'The environment is obviously something you feel strongly about.'

'Yes, but everyone is entitled to their own opinion,' Sophie countered, every inch of her body straining in an effort to be reasonable.

'That's not what you were saying earlier,' he commented.

James Harrison's eyebrows lifted, and for a moment she wondered if she saw the ghost of a smile in his eyes.

'I thought you were dead against the new supermarket complex,' he went on.

'I am,' Sophie replied with conviction, 'but there's no point in campaigning against something if your heart's not in it. And you made your feelings perfectly clear earlier this evening,' she added pointedly. 'This is it, here,' she said suddenly.

The car drew to a halt beside the terrace in

which Sophie had her apartment. For a few minutes after he had turned the engine off, there was silence. For some reason, Sophie felt strangely reluctant to move.

'I didn't say that I agreed with the developments,' James Harrison said quietly, 'just that it was important to consider both sides of the argument.'

In other words, he was implying that she was a hot-headed little fool who should look before she leaped!

'Well, you can't stay sitting on the fence for ever, you know,' Sophie said, her temper swiftly rising again. 'You'll have to make a decision sometime, before it's too late.'

'It's a very complex issue.'

James Harrison shook his head, refusing to be drawn.

'And I'm not in the habit of making snap decisions about important matters.'

'Well, then,' Sophie told him firmly, 'perhaps you need to take a fresh look at the beauty of the local countryside, to remind yourself of what you stand to lose if the development goes ahead.'

'This really means a lot to you, doesn't it?'

'Of course it does!' Sophie replied.

She looked away, unnerved by the intensity of his gaze. Suddenly it was as if the atmosphere in the car was charged with electricity. She wondered if James Harrison had felt it, too—the attraction that had pulsed between them when they looked into each other's eyes.

As if by some strange magnetism, Sophie found her gaze drawn back to his. Suddenly it seemed as though their faces were very close together within the confines of the car. His lips brushed hers before she knew what was happening. Instinctively Sophie leaned towards him, lulled by the sensuality of the caress into kissing him back.

When they drew apart, Sophie's cheeks flamed with embarrassment as she realised what she had done. It was her new colleague she had just kissed, her enemy, her adversary! Panicking, she fumbled for the car door.

'Thank you for the lift,' she blurted out, poised to make a quick getaway.

'Goodbye, Sophie,' James Harrison replied, his tone a strange mixture of disappointment and resignation, but Sophie didn't hear him— she was already gone.

He watched her slam the door shut before fleeing like a scalded cat. Trust him to have handled it all wrong as usual. He sighed as he turned the key in the ignition. His mouth twisted as he recalled the look on her face when she had realised who he was.

He had recognised her immediately as the firebrand from the supermarket, of course. Her whole persona was like a breath of fresh air. She had been sharp as a razor blade tonight at the meeting, and her conviction had

19

surprised him.

What was more, he didn't usually go round offering women lifts like that, but despite the prickly outside there had been a vulnerability about her that made him instinctively want to protect her. True, she had also irritated him, but in a way, he had enjoyed tussling with her tonight.

James Harrison shook his head, his face settling back into its customary frown as he manoeuvred the car away from the kerb. He didn't know what had got into him! He certainly hadn't meant to kiss her like that. He had moved down here to get away from all that sort of thing, to make a quiet, idyllic life for himself, just him and his woodwork, no relationships, no pressures, no complications.

Getting entangled with a woman hadn't been part of his plans, and he didn't intend to start changing them now.

Meanwhile, Sophie slammed her front door safely shut behind her, leaning back against it with a strange sense of relief. She ran tentative fingers over her still-tingling lips. Why had James Harrison kissed her like that? Their relationship hadn't exactly got off to the best of starts that evening!

Then she remembered that charge of attraction that had crackled between them. That kiss had been purely spontaneous, on her part at least. Well, she told herself firmly, next time she was in James Harrison's company she would have to be more wary.

She didn't intend starting any relationship with a man just now. She liked her life the way it was; liked her cosy, little flat, her friends, her painting and her work at Ecclesdon Crafts. And she was afraid that any involvement would threaten everything that she had achieved over the years.

CHAPTER TWO

'I wonder if that nice Mr Harrison is going to turn up tonight?' Mandy speculated aloud as they sat waiting for the meeting to start that Friday.

Sophie blushed at the very mention of his name.

'Talk about being the eternal optimist, Mandy!' she scoffed. 'James Harrison made his feelings perfectly clear at the meeting last Wednesday.'

'I don't know what got into you, Sophie, attacking the poor man like that.'

Mandy shook her head at the memory.

'If he doesn't turn up tonight, it'll probably be because you scared him off.'

'I don't know what got into me that night, either,' Sophie admitted, sighing. 'That man just rubbed me up the wrong way, I suppose.'

'Well, I thought he was dishy,' Mandy put in.

Sophie grimaced at her friend's choice of word.

'He is reasonably good-looking, I suppose,' she said grudgingly. 'It's just a shame he's so downright bad-tempered with it!'

'Anyone would have been, the way you were provoking him!' she exclaimed indignantly. 'Anyway,' she added with a smile, 'I like the strong, silent type. Oh, look! Here he comes!'

Mandy jumped out of her seat, waving till she had attracted the attention of the tall, dark figure at the back of the hall.

Sophie glanced over her shoulder. The town hall was packed. She had already seen several familiar faces amongst the rows of chairs, including Chris Atkins, who was a member of Ecclesdon Traders' Association. Waiting up on the stage with Steve Collins were the chairman of the traders' association, a representative of the supermarket chain, two council officers and a senior executive from the builders contracted to build the supermarket.

Sophie's heart had sunk as soon as Mandy had mentioned James Harrison's name. Why had he decided to come to the meeting tonight? It seemed unlikely that he had had a sudden change of heart and agreed to join their campaign, she thought, watching him thread his way towards them.

'Good evening Mandy, Sophie,' he said politely.

His greeting was curt and formal.

'So you decided to come after all,' she observed, leaning forward as James slid into the seat next to Mandy.

His eyes held hers for a long moment, reminding her uncomfortably of the kiss they had shared in his car. Sophie blushed, looking away.

'I never said I wouldn't come,' he answered eventually, turning away. 'Naturally I'm interested to hear both sides of the argument.'

It was over two hours later when the meeting broke up. Sophie's feelings were a mixture of disappointment and determination. They may have lost the battle, but she was determined they would win the war.

'Those councillors had no intention of listening to anything we said,' she commented indignantly to Mandy.

Mandy shook her head.

'I don't know why they bothered coming along tonight.'

Yet from the questions that had been asked during the meeting, it had become apparent that public opposition to the proposed developments was widespread. A vote had been held, and it had been decided that a protest would be held on the heath the following Monday, the day work was due to begin.

'At least we're taking some positive action,' Sophie consoled herself.

She caught up with James Harrison on his

way out.

'I noticed you abstained from the vote,' she remarked scathingly.

His reply took her aback.

'Since you already seem to have decided I'm your enemy,' he said coolly, 'I shouldn't think anything I do would surprise you any more.'

And with that, he turned on his heel and left.

*　　　*　　　*

'All set?' Sophie asked as Mandy got into her car on the Monday morning.

Mandy nodded.

'You know,' she said brightly, 'in a way I'm quite looking forward to today.'

'I hope you're not under the delusion that James Harrison is going to turn up.'

'Don't be an idiot, Sophie.'

Mandy looked serious for a moment.

'I care about saving the heath as much as you do, you know.'

Mandy kept up a steady stream of chatter while Sophie's old Ford Fiesta negotiated the narrow road, flanked by low, dry-stone walls. It was a drive Sophie always enjoyed, with green fields rolling to the east and, to the west, the land gently descending towards the distant, hazy sea.

As it was summer, the sky was already light,

and in early morning, the landscape looked somehow more lovely than ever. It made her stomach contract with anger to think that the beauty that surrounded her could be under threat.

When they arrived at the heath a few minutes later, it was still swathed in early-morning mist, but despite the earliness of the hour the area was already buzzing with activity. Sophie was greeted by several familiar faces, some fellow campaigners, some local tradespeople who feared for their livelihoods, and she also caught a glimpse of a busy, preoccupied-looking Steve Collins.

Amidst the crowd, they found Mary and Jean, and not far from them stood Tom.

'Hello, everyone,' Sophie greeted her fellow workers warmly. 'I'm so glad that you could all . . .'

Her sentence trailed off unfinished, for Steve Collins had climbed on to a grassy knoll, and was calling for everyone's attention. A striking figure with his mop of brown hair and patched dungarees, Steve outlined the morning's battle-plan.

'We've got to prevent the contractors from being able to begin their work, clearing this area of its beautiful trees and bushes,' he explained, his voice loud and clear through a megaphone.

A ripple of outrage travelled through the crowd at the thought of this.

'And how are we supposed to do that?' old Tom Bradley asked from somewhere nearby. 'I don't fancy my chances against a thirty-ton bulldozer.'

'We don't have to risk our lives!' Steve explained earnestly. 'The workmen are not allowed to touch us. All we have to do is get in their way, and hinder them doing their jobs.'

In the ensuing quiet Sophie could hear the low, distant rumble of heavy vehicles, gradually getting louder. Suddenly the crowd seemed restless, as if it had been spurred into action.

'Come on,' Sophie muttered to Mandy. 'Let's get ourselves settled before that lot arrives.'

All around them, people began to disperse quickly over the heath, the younger and more athletic ones climbing trees on the edge of the forest, the rest simply spreading themselves out on coats and blankets on the dewy grass. The first of the contractor's vehicles appeared around the corner of the road, a vast, lumbering convoy. A bulldozer rumbled on to the heath, coming to an abrupt halt about a hundred yards short of where they sat.

Sophie waved her placard as a thick-set man jumped down and came towards them.

'No Superstore on Ecclesdon Heath!' she shouted at him, her voice resonant with feeling, and some of the other protestors took up the chant.

By now a second subcontractor, a thin, wiry man, had joined the first.

'Do you people realise you're on private property?' he asked them.

As if in reply, the crowd chanted even louder.

'Come on, love,' the thick-set man said, coming towards Sophie. 'Move along now.'

'I'm not going anywhere!'

Her outer defiance hid an inner fear. Sophie knew he had no right to touch her, but she couldn't help shrinking away slightly as the big man came closer. She glanced anxiously around her. Where was Steve Collins when she needed him?

'We're only trying to do our job,' the other man told her, reasonably enough.

'Leave her alone,' someone said suddenly behind them.

The voice was low but unmistakably menacing. Everyone turned round to see who had spoken.

'James!'

Sophie blinked and looked again, but she wasn't seeing things. James Harrison stood there large as life, looking, as Sophie realised to her discomfort, devastatingly attractive in a faded green cotton shirt and long, stone-coloured shorts.

What was he doing here, she wondered incredulously. She averted her gaze from his muscular calves and tanned knees. With an

27

effort she wrenched her mind back to her present predicament.

Something in James's voice must have told the workman he meant business. Instantly he raised both hands in a gesture of surrender.

'All right, mate, all right! I wasn't going to do her any harm!' he said hastily, backing away from Sophie.

As soon as the men had retreated, Sophie's fighting spirit returned to her. She rounded on James.

'What are you doing here?'

'Well, that's a charming greeting, I must say.'

'I mean, I thought you disapproved of our demonstration.'

'I never said that.'

'Oh, and by the way,' she added, 'I'm quite capable of looking after myself, thank you!'

'You could have fooled me,' he muttered sarcastically. 'You were cowering just then like a frightened puppy!'

'I was not!'

'You were.'

He glanced disparagingly towards the workmen, then back at Sophie.

'I can't blame you. It was hardly a fair contest, two strong men against one woman.'

'Just because I'm a woman, it doesn't mean I'm incapable of sticking up for myself!' Sophie hissed.

'I was brought up to believe that a man

should look after a woman,' he replied coldly.

Sophie shook her head in disbelief.

'In case you haven't noticed, we're not living in the middle ages any more. Nowadays a woman likes to have at least some small measure of independence!'

'I'll remember that next time you're being molested by thugs.'

James Harrison raised his eyebrows meaningfully, and Sophie flushed indignantly, but she had no time to think up a suitable retort. More men were climbing out of vehicles now and she vented her frustration by chanting more loudly than ever, joined by others.

'Do you really think it's wise to encourage this sort of behaviour?' he asked her, his irritation thinly concealed.

Gazing back at him, Sophie was plunged into confusion. One minute James Harrison was rushing to defend her, the next he was acting if she had done something wrong. But perhaps, a more sensible voice in her head reasoned, if they refused to rise to the bait offered by the contractors, some sort of dialogue could be established. It was probably the only chance they had if they were going to save Ecclesdon Heath. The foreman was now threatening to call the police!

'Go on, then!' a voice called rebelliously from the trees behind them.

To her disappointment, she recognised the

voice as belonging to Steve Collins. Cries of approval soon echoed around the heath.

The foreman shrugged defeatedly before motioning to his men to retreat. The fifteen or so workers gathered together, speaking in low voices so that Sophie was unable to distinguish what was being said.

'If only both sides could sit down and discuss the situation like sensible adults!' she said exasperatedly to Mandy. 'I'm sure that if we could just talk to these men we could make them see how wrong it is to destroy such a beautiful piece of countryside.'

'I couldn't agree more.'

To Sophie's surprise it was James Harrison who had spoken, from where he sat on the grass nearby.

'About the discussion, that is,' he qualified. 'Whether they'd be instantly converted to your point of view is another matter.'

Sophie decided to take this as an insult rather than a compliment, and flashed him an indignant look. To her discomfort, he met the look and their eyes locked for several seconds.

'Unfortunately, there's nothing either sensible or adult about these people!' Mandy put in, oblivious to the undercurrents of tension running between Sophie and James. 'Anyone want a sandwich?' she added, producing a large sandwich box from her holdall and handing it round.

They munched in silence for a couple of

30

minutes, enjoying a well-earned break from their chanting. The sun was growing warm on their faces.

'So,' Mandy said, fixing James with her most alluring smile, 'what made you decide to uproot yourself from Croydon and move down to the West Country?'

'Like I said, I love the countryside.'

James seemed as reluctant as ever to answer questions about himself. Then his eyes suddenly softened, as if at some fond memory.

'We used to come to Dorset for family holidays, when I was a child.'

'Are you an only child?'

In spite of herself, Sophie was intrigued to learn more about this elusive man.

James shook his head.

'I've got a younger sister, Susan.'

From the sound of his voice, he was clearly very fond of his little sister.

'She's got a family of her own now, but she still lives in Croydon, near my mother. My father died some years ago.'

'So you'd always dreamed of moving down here,' Sophie mused, guiltily remembering how she had accused him of not caring about the area.

James nodded briefly.

'And last year I finally decided the time had come to make a move. I knew it was now or never—'

Suddenly he broke off abruptly, his eyes on

a point beyond Sophie's left shoulder.

'Where's Mary going?' he muttered tersely under his breath.

Sophie glanced round, her gaze drawn to Mary's tall, thin figure, as she made her way towards one of the contractor's vehicles. Sophie frowned.

'Surely she isn't about to offer an unconditional surrender to the workmen?'

The next moment Sophie's frown deepened as she saw Mary prising the petrol cap off one of the vehicles and proceeding to pour what looked like water from a drinking bottle into the fuel tank.

'It looks more like she's attempting to sabotage one of the contractors' vehicles,' James said grimly.

'Surely she wouldn't do something so stupid?' Sophie whispered. She felt a surge of anger. She had always believed Mary to be a respectable, middle-aged woman.

'I don't know,' James muttered. 'But I'm about to find out.'

Before Sophie knew what was happening, James Harrison had leaped to his feet and was striding across to intercept Mary as she returned to her position. Instinctively Sophie got to her feet, too, her feelings for once echoing James's own.

'What do you think you're doing?' James challenged Mary, his voice ominously low and controlled.

Mary looked surprised, but quickly recovered herself.

'All's fair in love and war,' she retorted, a glint in her eyes that Sophie had never seen before.

'But you're causing criminal damage,' James pointed out to her. 'Possibly hundreds of pounds' worth. Do you realise what would happen if you got caught?'

Mary gave James a look of disgust.

'Sophie was right!' she snorted derisively, 'You don't care about our countryside at all—well,' she went on, raising her voice, 'we're sick of outsiders coming along and telling us what's best for us!'

'Hear, hear!'

Raucous cries of approval met Mary's comment, and people nearby, with Sophie's and Mandy's stunned exceptions, began to chant again. But this time they directed their words at James, as if he personally was responsible for their grievances.

'I think you're all being totally unreasonable about this!'

Anger glinted in James Harrison's dark eyes and his fists clenched at his sides as he responded to their actions.

He had to shout to make himself heard above the chanting. His glance swept across Sophie. Their eyes met, and it seemed in that instant that he was including her in his disapproval. Something inside her cringed

33

away from the derision in his eyes, At once any sympathy she had for him vanished, to be replaced by indignant anger.

'You're the one who's being unreasonable!' Sophie flung back at him. 'Making assumptions, and tarring everyone with the same brush!'

James Harrison's mouth settled into an angry line.

'I knew it would be a mistake coming here today.'

He glowered at her.

'Well, why did you bother, then?' Sophie retorted, stung by his undeserved disapproval. Impulsively she added, 'It would have been better for everyone if you'd stayed at home!'

James's head jerked back towards her. A flicker of hurt passed through his eyes. For a moment Sophie experienced a pang of regret, wishing she could take her thoughtless words back.

'I'm going,' he said shortly. 'Do you want a lift?'

'No thank you,' Sophie replied coldly. 'I'll stay to see this through!'

The chanting around them had reached a crescendo. Sophie saw that the police had arrived. The next few minutes passed in a blur. Suddenly people were on their feet and Sophie got to her feet, too, fearful that she would be trampled.

Then the crowd surged towards the

defensive line of policemen. Sophie found herself borne forward on a sea of bodies and placards, unable to move of her own volition.

'Mandy!'

Panicking, she scanned the crowd for her friend, but she was nowhere to be seen.

Then suddenly Sophie was knocked to the ground, her scream lost in the general noise. It seemed to Sophie as though everything was closing in around her and she raised her arms to protect herself from the forest of trampling legs. Then everything went mercifully dark.

CHAPTER THREE

The next thing Sophie knew, she was being lifted to safety by a pair of strong, muscular arms. Looking up, she wondered if she was seeing things when she looked straight into the face of James Harrison.

He was intent on pushing his way through the crowd, however, and Sophie instinctively pressed her face closer to his warm, broad chest, seeking protection from the bodies that jostled around them.

Eventually they reached safety away from the crowd, and he placed her gently down on the grass at the edge of the heath, the expression in his eyes unreadable.

Sophie raised her head and tried to speak.

35

'Don't tell me you're perfectly capable of looking after yourself!' he said gruffly.

Sophie shook her head and sank back on to the ground, momentarily too weak to talk. Her whole body was trembling, though whether from the shock of her experience or from the recent contact with James Harrison's warm, muscular body, she was unable to tell.

'I thought you'd gone,' she admitted weakly, when she could eventually speak again.

'I'm glad I didn't,' he said in a low voice. 'I don't know what might have happened to you if I hadn't heard you scream.'

Sophie grimaced, remembering the forest of legs around her, and the terrifying feeling that she was about to be crushed to death. She owed a lot, possibly her life, to James Harrison.

'Thank you—James,' she said.

She spoke his name tentatively, her voice little more than a whisper. Sophie wondered if she was suffering from concussion. Suddenly James Harrison's craggy face had softened and the look in his eyes was almost tender. The next moment she was sure she must be imagining it as he leaned down, kissing her gently on the lips.

The kiss deepened as Sophie responded, lasting for what seemed like several minutes but must have been only seconds. For a moment the world around her disappeared. What was happening, she wondered dazedly.

She had never felt like this before.

Drawing away, James Harrison wondered what had got into him, kissing her like that. The truth was that he had been more shaken up than he cared to admit at the thought of what might have happened to Sophie if he hadn't been there to rescue her.

His first impressions had been confirmed—beneath the outer show of toughness and independence, she was gentle and vulnerable. He had been so relieved when he found her that he had just wanted to crush her to him, to keep her safe from any further harm.

James had never felt like that before—in the past he had never allowed a woman to get too close, and at heart he had remained a confirmed bachelor. Perhaps that was why he was at a loss as to what to do next.

*   *   *

'Hello, Sophie! How nice to see you again.'

Sophie, deep in contemplation of the supermarket shelves, almost jumped out of her skin.

'Chris!' she exclaimed, turning round.

To her surprise, he seemed genuinely pleased to see her.

Sophie had dropped Mandy off before heading back towards the town centre. She had one or two things to pick up at the supermarket and besides, after the drama of the morning she felt she needed to get back in touch with reality again.

She had been locking the car when suddenly she remembered that kiss. She hadn't imagined it, had she? That this time there had been more to the kiss than just physical attraction? She wondered whether it was just her, or if James had felt it, too.

After that things had happened quickly. The police had managed to bring the crowd under control, and most of the protesters had agreed to go quietly home. Sophie, now fully recovered from her ordeal, had accepted that they had no option.

After all, they had achieved their purpose in preventing work being carried out on the heath that day. Mary Howard had, however, physically resisted the attempts of the policemen to move her on, and as a result had been bundled off to the local police station.

'You weren't at the protest today, then?' she commented now to Chris.

He shook his head regretfully.

'I must say I'm surprised,' Sophie admitted. 'After all, your business would be ruined if the new supermarket went ahead.'

Briefly she told Chris about that morning's events, leaving out the bit about her being rescued by James Harrison.

'Why don't you come along and join us one day?' she finished. 'It might be in your interests.'

'It's not really my scene you know, hanging around with the tree people.'

Chris looked doubtful.

'It's all quite respectable and above board, really!' Sophie laughed.

She had to admit that he had a point, though. It was hard to envisage Chris, immaculate in his suit, with his neat, slicked-back hair, waving a placard and chanting on the heath.

'Think about it, though,' she urged him. 'After all, you could stand to lose more than most of us.'

'I will.'

Chris lowered his voice, gesturing at the shelves around him.

'There's no way a little place like this could compete with the sort of thing they're proposing.'

'I know.' Sophie shook her head sadly in agreement.

'Let's face it,' Chris went on earnestly, 'small town-centre stores like this have had their day. The out-of-town supermarket complexes are clearly the way of the future.'

'I don't know how you can be so objective about it all, Chris,' she commented. 'Anyway, perhaps I'll see you at the heath some time in the future.'

'Actually, Sophie,' Chris said suddenly, 'there was something else I wanted to ask you.'

'What is it, Chris?' Sophie frowned, puzzled.

'You must realise you're a very attractive lady, Sophie,' he said in a low voice, his eyes flickering appreciatively over her. 'I—I'd very much like to take you out to dinner some time.'

'Dinner? Me?'

Sophie could scarcely suppress her surprise. She'd never thought of Chris as anything other than a friend before, and assumed he felt the same about her. It was a few moments before she could gather her wits sufficiently to respond.

'Thank you for the compliment, Chris, but I'm afraid my answer must be "no",' she said, as gently as she could.

'Why not, Sophie?' Chris looked as if he couldn't believe she had turned him down.

The question hung unanswered in the air as Sophie gazed at the young man's smooth face, as if seeking the answer there. Although Chris's name had been linked with one or two local girls in the past, none of his relationships had lasted.

Chris was certainly an eligible young man, and her parents liked him, so why did Sophie's instincts tell her to decline his invitation? The realisation that it was because of James Harrison came as something of a shock to her.

'I—I'm just not ready for a relationship at the moment,' Sophie fudged.

That, at least, was the truth. She hadn't meant to get involved with a man, so why was she unable to suppress her feelings for James Harrison?

'I can't say I'm not disappointed, Sophie.'

Chris's frustration was evident in his sigh. Then suddenly he became brisk and businesslike once more.

'But, anyway, duty calls.'

He gave her a parting smile.

'I'll warn you though, Sophie, I don't give up easily on something I want.'

*   *   *

Sophie dipped her brush into the pool of green water, wiping off the excess moisture on the side of the palette. Then she returned to the artist's pad in front of her, gently stroking the palest of washes within the faint, curving pencil outline of a leaf.

She almost jumped out of her skin when the phone in the hall jangled into life.

'Hi, Sophie. It's me.'

Mandy's voice sounded breathlessly and excitable down the phone. As her friend had been working at the craft shop that morning she had been unable to attend today's demonstration. Fortunately Steve Collins had, with typical thoroughness, drawn up a rota, ensuring that there were some protesters present at the heath all the time.

'Well, how did it go today?' Mandy asked. 'What happened to Mary?'

41

'The police let her off with a warning this time,' Sophie explained, getting the feeling that her friend wasn't really listening. 'And she phoned up James Harrison and apologised to him.'

Sophie did not add that this had been her idea.

'I just hope she isn't stupid enough to do the same thing again.' She sighed in a long-suffering way. 'Mandy, I've known you long enough to be able to tell when you've got something on your mind. What is it?'

Mandy gave a breathless sigh.

'You'll never guess what happened, Soph. James came into the shop in the afternoon shift today, and I was showing him the ropes, seeing as it was his first day, and we got chatting and—well, the long and short of it is that I'm going out for a drink with him this evening!'

'Oh.'

Sophie was aware that Mandy was still gabbling on excitedly, but she heard nothing of what her friend said.

How could he? All she could think of was how he had kissed her, and the tenderness in his eyes. After what happened between them, how could he turn his attentions to her best friend?

'Sophie?' Mandy was prompting now. 'Aren't you excited for me?'

'Of course I am, Mandy.'

42

Sophie made an effort to snap out of her apathy.

'So, have you decided what you're going to wear yet?'

After rambling happily on for a few minutes, Mandy said, 'Anyway, I must go and get ready—I want to make sure I'm looking my best tonight.'

'Yes, of course. 'Bye, Mandy.'

After Sophie had put down the phone, she wandered through the house in a trance-like state. For the rest of the evening she dabbed listlessly at her watercolour, but for once her work failed to absorb her, the easy rhythm of her life disrupted. Even when she went to bed she tossed and turned, unable to banish the thought of James Harrison and Mandy from her mind.

*   *   *

The following morning, it was Sophie's turn to work at the craft shop and she showered and dressed in a cool, summer dress, tossing her patchwork rucksack casually over her shoulder.

Yet for once as she strolled down the gently inclining road into the town she was oblivious to the spectacular view of Ecclesdon Bay, with the Purbeck Hills rolling in the distance and the blue sea shimmering in the heat of another perfect summer's day.

She was glad that the tourist season was getting under way and there was a steady trickle of customers passing through the craft shop that morning. After only an hour she had sold one of Mandy's dried flower arrangements, a couple of Mary's chunky, pottery mugs and one of Tom's oil paintings—a stunning view of Ecclesdon Bay at sunset.

And any minute now, if she was lucky, she was going to sell one of her framed flower watercolours to a sweet, elderly couple. Sure enough, the old lady pointed to the painting, while her husband offered the money.

'So pretty, dear,' the lady said to Sophie. 'Did you paint it yourself?'

Before the old couple left they both signed the petition Sophie had placed on the desk, saying that although they were only visitors to the area they felt it would be a crime to spoil the lovely local scenery. Sophie was positioning another of her watercolours in place of the one she had sold when she heard a noise behind her.

'Just a moment, I'll be right with you,' she called without looking round, thinking it was a customer.

'Oh, I shouldn't put yourself out on my behalf, Sophie,' James Harrison's voice answered lightly.

'James!' she exclaimed, returning to her seat behind the desk. 'You gave me a shock.'

She spoke quickly, to cover her confused

feelings at seeing him again. Despite her anger with him, not to mention her feeling that he had betrayed her, Sophie couldn't deny the pleasure that surged within her at the sight of the familiar tall figure with its tousled brown hair and deep brown eyes, clad in a T-shirt and faded jeans.

'What are you doing here?' she asked, her heart pounding rapidly.

'I'm just restocking my display,' he told her, gesturing towards a large crate on the floor beside him. 'I had a good day yesterday— beginner's luck, I suppose. You don't mind, do you?' he added.

'No, of course not.'

Trust James Harrison to choose today to be unusually friendly! What had got into him? She wished he would hurry up and get on with what he had come here to do, so that she could be left alone to sort out her confused thoughts. Even when he had lugged his crate over to his own display area she was not to be left in peace, however.

'Not at the demonstration today then?' he asked conversationally, unpacking a batch of ash and mahogany pot-plant stands.

'I would have thought that was obvious.'

As soon as she had spoken, Sophie bit her lip. It wasn't like her to be sarcastic. Her bad night's sleep must be catching up on her.

James abandoned his work temporarily and strolled across to the area where Sophie's pale, delicate, framed watercolours were displayed. Sophie watched him uneasily. The longer he stared, the more uncomfortable she felt. It was as if some secret, inner part of her had been laid bare to his scrutiny. And in spite of herself, Sophie hung on his approval.

'Very pretty,' he commented eventually.

'Pretty?'

To Sophie's over-sensitive ears, it sounded very much as though she was being damned with faint praise.

'Is that the best you can say?' she asked indignantly.

'Fishing for compliments, Sophie?'

To her annoyance, the corners of James' mouth curled with mocking amusement.

Sophie blushed furiously.

'Of course not!' she muttered under her breath.

She was aware that he was teasing her, amusing himself at her expense, but why?

Well, two could play at that game! Mimicking his nonchalance, Sophie strolled from behind the desk to the area where James's own crafts were displayed. She picked up a richly-coloured mahogany bowl, turning it carefully over in her hands.

'I suppose you realise that by using this wood you're contributing to the destruction of the South American rainforests,' she said casually.

James shook his head, meeting her gaze

levelly.

'Actually, I only use hardwoods that come from replanted forests.'

'Oh.'

Sophie was relieved, of course, but she also had to admit that she was taken aback.

'Surprised, Sophie?' he asked her, eyebrows raised.

'Well, yes,' she confessed. 'I—I didn't think you'd be bothered about things like that,' given your lukewarm attitude to saving Ecclesdon Heath, she added mentally.

'Well,' he replied firmly, 'I am.'

At that moment their exchange was cut short by the jangle of the shop bell, heralding the arrival of a couple of customers. Sophie exchanged polite greetings with the two women but her eyes were on James as he swept past with his empty crate. She tried to banish her illogical disappointment at the thought that he might not return.

'We'll take these, thank you.'

After browsing for several minutes, the two women handed over some of Sophie's flower notelets and a set of James's wooden coasters.

At that moment James returned, staggering under the weight of another loaded crate. Sophie quickly finished wrapping the coasters.

'What's this?'

One of the women pointed to Sophie's petition.

'It's a petition to save Ecclesdon Heath,'

47

Sophie explained. 'Have you heard that they're proposing to build a supermarket on the site?'

She was only too keen to elaborate on the plight of the heath, and felt a thrill of achievement when the two women added their signatures. When the customers had gone, James came over to the desk and scrutinised the petition.

'Do you want to sign it?' Sophie asked him, never one to miss an opportunity. 'I've got a pen.'

'I think I'll take a raincheck on it for the time being,' he muttered, still scrutinising the document. 'Thanks all the same.'

He was doing it again, criticising her in a way that made her feel strangely vulnerable. Why did this man have the power to make her doubt her feelings, her opinions, everything that she held dear?

'I knew you weren't on our side over this,' she flung at him, inexplicably angry, 'right from the start!'

'What do you mean?' James looked stunned at her outburst.

'You were reluctant to become involved in saving the heath from the word go!' she exclaimed.

'I came along to the protest, didn't I?'

'Yes, but only so that you could give us all a lecture on how we should be behaving. And now this!'

She stabbed an angry finger at the petition.

'I'm not sure this is the appropriate place for that petition, Sophie.' He frowned. 'People do come in here for pleasure, after all.'

This was the final straw for Sophie.

'What's the matter with you, James?' she said indignantly. 'Don't you care about your local countryside?'

'What's the matter with me?'

James stepped towards her, suddenly angry.

'I come in here today and you treat me as if I'm something you detest.'

'I have not!'

'Don't try and deny it.'

He grabbed her by her wrists, forcing her to meet his eyes, his own gaze dark and unwavering.

'All morning you've been spoiling for a fight, Sophie,' he told her, his voice low but threatening. 'Now I think I've got a right to know just what's going on!'

'Let go of me!'

Pulling her wrists free of his grasp, Sophie stopped for the first time to assess her feelings. Perhaps James was right. She was upset about his attitude towards saving the heath, but, if she was honest, there was more to it than that. Such as the fact that he had gone out with her best friend last night . . .

'If you must know, James,' she said self-righteously, rubbing her wrists, 'I'm disappointed in you.'

To her surprise he just shrugged.

'You've said yourself that everyone's entitled to their own opinion.'

'I'm not talking about that, I'm talking about the fact that you went out with Mandy yesterday,' she blurted.

As soon as she had spoken, it struck Sophie how feeble the accusation sounded.

'Is that all?'

To her chagrin, James actually laughed.

'All?' she echoed indignantly, aware she was blushing.

Instantly his laughter died.

'Mandy and I are just friends, you know,' he said quietly.

'Like us, I suppose?' Sophie challenged.

As soon as she had spoken she regretted it. She had no claim on this man, just because he had kissed her, especially considering they had both probably been overcome by shock at the time.

'It's the truth.' He shrugged. 'Take it or leave it.'

'I don't believe you.'

With Mandy's slender figure and pretty face, Sophie defied any man to be interested in her simply as a friend. Sophie frowned. She had never had cause to be jealous of her friend's looks before.

'You know, I'm disappointed in you, too,' James said, after a brief pause.

'Why?' Sophie asked, stung by his words.

'I thought you really cared about saving the

environment.'

'I do!' she protested.

James looked disbelieving.

'It seems to me you're more bothered by the possibility that I might be having a relationship with your best friend.'

When Sophie opened her mouth to protest, James shook his head.

'That was what I really liked about you, Sophie,' he said seriously, 'Your complete lack of—of pettiness, and your devotion to the things that really mattered.'

'James, I . . .' Sophie felt shamed by his words.

'Yes, Sophie?'

He turned back towards her.

She wanted to tell him that she was sorry for the way she had behaved today but, somehow, the words stuck in her throat.

'Nothing,' she murmured.

After giving her one final, disappointed glance, James went back to his work in stony silence.

CHAPTER FOUR

'Fancy going for a drink this evening?' Sophie asked Mandy a couple of days later.

They were at the craft shop—Mandy had worked the morning shift, while Sophie had arrived to do the afternoon.

When her friend hesitated, Sophie frowned. Was it her imagination, or had Mandy been less friendly than usual over the last couple of days?

'Only it seems ages since we had a chance for a proper chat, what with the demonstrations and everything,' Sophie added persuasively.

Mandy had been at the protest on the heath the previous day but it was hardly surprising that they had had little chance to talk. To Sophie's relief, her friend seemed to relent.

'I know,' Mandy suggested, 'why don't you come round to me? We could crack open a bottle of wine.'

'That would be great, Mandy.'

Sophie smiled warmly at her friend, for a moment almost forgetting her ulterior motives. She didn't normally angle for invitations like this, but ever since Mandy had gone out with James, Sophie had been dying to ask her about it, and it seemed as though tonight she would finally get the opportunity.

Later, when Sophie was relaxing in Mandy's living-room, a glass of sparkling wine in her hand, she sat up suddenly as if the thought had just occurred to her.

'You never did tell me how your date with James went! Come on, Mandy, I want to know all the gory details.'

The truth was that it would be torture to

Sophie to hear all the details, but it was a form of torture she was unable to resist inflicting on herself.

Mandy topped up their glasses before answering.

'You know, Sophie,' she said slowly, handing her a glass, 'I got the feeling he only agreed to go for a drink with me so he could cross-question me about you.'

Sophie shook her head dismissively.

'He wouldn't have asked you out if he wasn't interested in you, Mandy.'

'I never said he asked me out. I asked him out, actually.'

'But I thought . . .' Sophie's eyes widened in disbelief.

'I was fed up with waiting for him to make the first move.'

A sobering thought smothered Sophie's surprise.

'But he still wouldn't have agreed to go if he didn't like you, Mandy,' she said softly.

'I did ask him purely on a friendly basis.' When Sophie raised her eyebrows she added defensively, 'It was the only way I could get him to agree!'

Sophie's heart leaped in sudden realisation. So James hadn't betrayed her after all! Then she noticed the way her friend was looking at her, and her heart sank again.

'I'm sorry things didn't work out between you and James,' Sophie said slowly, meeting her friend's eyes.

Mandy shrugged.

'You might have told me there was something going on between you and him.'

Her blue eyes were reproachful, and Sophie sensed that this was the reason behind her friend's recent coolness.

'There's nothing going on between us, Mandy.'

A hot blush seeped across Sophie's cheeks.

'James Harrison can't stand the sight of me.'

Mandy shook her head.

'Believe me,' she said grimly, 'he definitely likes you.'

For a moment she sounded almost resentful. Then her tone lightened slightly.

'The question is, do you like him?'

Sophie's blush deepened. Suddenly she couldn't keep up the pretence any longer. The fact that she disagreed with his opinions over the heath didn't seem to matter any more. She wasn't sure what she felt for James Harrison but she could no longer feign indifference.

'I don't know, Mandy. But the way I spoke to James a couple of days ago,' she admitted, 'I think I've ruined the chances of any sort of relationship developing between us.'

'Sophie, you are hopeless!' Mandy exploded, reverting to her usual self.

She grinned suddenly, and Sophie grinned back, sensing that a truce had been established between them.

'Well, you'll just have to make it up to him, won't you?'

'Make it up to him?' Sophie asked hesitantly, the smile fading from her lips. 'How do I do that?'

Mandy thought for a moment. 'It's the craft fair next Sunday, so you'll have the ideal opportunity then. You'll just have to use every one of your feminine wiles to try and persuade him that you didn't mean whatever it was you said!'

The following Sunday found the two friends making their way to the local fair. Sophie wasn't at all sure if the opportunity to apologise to James would present itself that day or even that she agreed with Mandy it was the best thing to do.

'What if he's not there?'

Sophie mused anxiously as she manoeuvred the car into a parking space on the sea-front. Following Mandy's advice, she had dressed with care, in her flowing blue patchwork skirt and embroidered white blouse, her auburn hair hanging loose around her shoulders.

'Of course he'll be there,' Mandy answered briskly. 'He's a craftsman, isn't he?'

Mandy was right. Despite the fact that they were early, James was among the stallholders who had already arrived at the seafront pavilion and were setting out their wares. Mary Howard had the stall next to his.

'I'm glad to see those two seem to have

resolved their differences,' Sophie whispered.

But Mandy was not to be deflected from her purpose.

'Go on,' she hissed. 'Take the table the other side of James. I'll have the one next to you.'

When Sophie hesitated anxiously, Mandy gave her a sharp nudge in the ribs, sending her reeling in James's direction.

'Hello, Mary. Hello, James.'

She smiled brightly, putting her box of wares on the table.

At first James seemed surprised to see her there but he quickly recovered himself, however.

'Hello, Sophie,' he replied curtly.

Sophie's heart sank. So he was back to his old, surly self.

Within a few minutes, Sophie had spread her lace cloth over her stall and begun to arrange her paintings. It was not long before she realised that she was going to run out of room. Gratefully, she pounced on a small, round table that seemed to be going spare.

'Where are you going with that?' A familiar voice demanded suddenly.

Sophie spun round, coming face to face with James.

'I just thought, as no-one seemed to need it . . .'

'That's not just any old table—it's a James Harrison exclusive!' he said indignantly. 'In future, why don't you ask before you take something that doesn't belong to you?'

'I'm sorry,' Sophie said, blushing. 'Here, have your table back.'

'Forget it,' James muttered. 'You might as well use it. But if anyone enquires about it, tell them it's for sale at sixty pounds.'

Grudgingly he came over to help her move it.

'Where do you want it?'

'Here, please.'

Penitently, Sophie indicated the space to the right of her stall.

'You can't have it there.'

'Why not?' she asked, as mildly as she could, determined not to let him get to her.

'Because it's blocking the fire exit.'

Sophie frowned at her stall, but decided to let him put the table where he wanted—the last thing she wanted was a stand up fight in the middle of the hall.

As soon as the doors were opened a stream of visitors surged in, and did not abate all morning. Sophie was so busy that she scarcely had time to think about James Harrison. She had placed a petition defiantly on the corner of her stall, and several customers stopped to sign it.

Only when lunchtime arrived was there a slight lull. Sophie was enjoying a rest and her sandwiches so much that for a moment she didn't notice a couple hovering in front of her stall.

'Mum, Dad!' she exclaimed suddenly, jumping up. 'It seems ages since I've seen you,' she murmured, hugging them both.

Seeing their familiar, well-loved faces, Sophie felt a pang of guilt. She knew she should make an effort to visit more often, especially as they only lived just outside Ecclesdon.

'Mum, Dad, you know Mandy already,' then turning to her right she said, 'and this is my— er, colleague, James Harrison.'

She blushed as she spoke.

'Pleased to met you, Mr and Mrs Taylor.'

James smiled across at them, uncharacteristically amiable. Sophie blinked, wondering for a moment if she was seeing things.

'How's the fair going?' her father asked.

'It's going really well. I'm sure there are twice as many people as last year.'

Sophie enthused for a few moments about the number of paintings she had sold. The conversation inevitably turned to the proposed supermarket. Naturally her parents had heard about the protests on the heath—the local papers had been full of it.

'Are you sure it's safe?' her mother asked anxiously.

'Of course it is, Mum. You two ought to join us one day,' she told both her parents earnestly. 'I know how much the two of you love the local countryside.'

Out of the corner of her eye Sophie caught a glimpse of James Harrison's face, and it seemed to her that he looked amused. She felt a sudden glimmer of hope. Could it be that he was beginning to relent towards her?

Sophie's father caught James's eye.

'Our Sophie's on her soap-box again,' he said fondly, sharing the other man's amusement. 'She's always been the same, even when she was a little girl . . .'

'Dad!' Sophie interrupted furiously, her eyes flashing a warning to him.

Unfortunately her mother was unaware of the exchange of looks.

'Yes, she always did know her own mind, even when she was a toddler,' she continued happily.

Sophie flushed, wishing her mother would stop talking.

'Really?' James asked, listening politely.

'Mum, I'm sure no-one wants to hear this stuff.'

'No, do go on, Mrs Taylor,' James said with a sideways glance at Sophie. 'It's quite fascinating.'

Then, just when it seemed things couldn't get any worse, Sophie saw Chris Atkins, making a bee-line for her stall, looking immaculate even in a casual shirt and trousers. She frowned—Chris was the last person she wanted to see right at that moment. Aghast, she watched him glance at James and saw their eyes lock in mutual recognition.

'Hello, Sophie, how are you?' he greeted her, holding out a hand. He turned to her parents. 'Richard, Jane, what a pleasant surprise!'

Unlike Sophie, her parents were delighted to see Chris and chatted for a good ten minutes.

'We'll go and have a look round now, and leave you young people in peace,' Sophie's father said presently.

He winked meaningfully at Sophie and Chris.

'I'm sure you two have got plenty to talk about!'

Sophie was horrified.

'No, don't rush off Mum, Dad!' she protested.

But her protests were in vain.

'We'll be back later,' her mother promised as they left.

Sophie flushed uncomfortably. She knew that both her parents liked Chris. They had probably both been hoping for years that he and Sophie would get together.

'Shall we go and get some lunch?' Chris asked her casually. 'Your father was right— we've do have plenty to talk about.'

'Chris, I'd love to, but . . .' Sophie searched for an excuse, desperate to be rid of him.

Suddenly James Harrison had strode over,

and was standing beside them.

'Actually,' James said, his tone icy cold, 'she's having lunch with me.'

He placed a proprietorial hand on Sophie's wrist. His dark gaze challenged Chris Atkins to contradict him, but it seemed that for once the younger man was lost for words.

'Come on,' James barked.

Bemused, Sophie allowed herself to be manoeuvred deftly in the direction of the adjoining bar and restaurant, leaving Chris Atkins staring speechlessly after them. As soon as they were safely in the bar, James relinquished his hold on her.

'Now, can I get you a drink while we study the menu?' he asked, suddenly as courteous as if this was any normal lunch date.

'Oh—yes, an orange juice, please,' Sophie murmured.

She was confused by James's behaviour. All morning he had been virtually ignoring her, so why was he suddenly showing such an interest in her? Still unsure what was going on, she followed him to a secluded table by one of the large windows with a picturesque view of the waves breaking on the shore.

'Now, what was all that about?' Sophie asked after she had taken a sustaining sip of her orange juice.

Her tone was indignant, but secretly she could not deny her pleasure that James had gone to such trouble to stop her having lunch with Chris.

'I don't know.'

James had the grace to look shame-faced.

'I shouldn't have acted like that. It's just that—well—you deserve better than Atkins, Sophie.'

'Are you trying to imply that Chris Atkins and I are an item?'

'I'm not trying to imply anything. I'm sorry. I spoke out of turn just now. Your relationship with Atkins is none of my business.'

'What relationship? Chris and I are just friends, you know!' Sophie protested indignantly.

James raised his eyebrows.

'Well, he certainly doesn't seem to think so,' he remarked drily.

'What Chris thinks has got nothing to do with it!' Sophie retorted.

'And neither did your parents, for that matter,' James went on, unable to stop himself now that he was into his flow. 'It looked to me as though they viewed Atkins very much as a future son-in-law. Though why they'd want to marry off their daughter to that jumped-up little pipsqueak . . .'

'What?'

Suddenly Sophie was speechless with indignation. James Harrison might be many things, but it wasn't like him to be downright rude. Suddenly she had had enough. So much for Mandy's good advice! There was only so much grovelling her pride could take.

'I'm not going to sit here and listen to you insulting not only my friends, but my parents, too!' she burst out, scraping back her chair and getting abruptly to her feet.

There was an ominous break in his voice and she could feel that tears were threatening. Then, before she was tempted to tip her orange juice over his head, she turned and all but ran from the restaurant.

CHAPTER FIVE

Half-blinded by unshed tears, Sophie almost bumped into the large, capable figure of Jean as the older woman walked into the bar.

'Sophie!' Jean exclaimed, beaming. 'Just the girl I was looking for!'

Sophie cursed mentally. This was all she needed.

'We need models for the fashion show at three,' Jean was continuing. 'Can you help us out?'

Sophie racked her brain for some excuse. The idea of parading around in fancy clothes watched by a crowd of people sounded like torture to her, especially the way she felt at the moment. But, a voice reasoned, Jean and the others had been very supportive over saving the heath.

'Go on, Sophie,' Jean coaxed. 'It'll be fun.'

'Oh, all right, then,' Sophie said reluctantly.

'Good girl!' Jean beamed at her. 'I knew you wouldn't let us down. Ah, James and Mike.'

Looking up, Sophie saw that James had returned to the bar, where he was sipping his pint of beer and chatting to Mike Barratt, a well-known local silversmith. Sophie glanced down as James looked across.

'You two will offer your services as models, won't you?' Jean urged.

'You've talked me into it.' Mike grinned, turning to James. 'What about you, mate?'

'I really don't think . . .' James began curtly.

'Of course he will!' Mike interrupted, oblivious to James glowering darkly in the background.

Later, Sophie followed Mandy reluctantly to the pavilion's backstage dressing-rooms.

'Relax, Sophie,' Mandy told her. 'You'll enjoy it once you get into the swing of it.'

Sophie looked unconvinced. A few minutes later, a long-haired woman, whom Sophie vaguely recognised from onc of the other stalls, thrust a scrap of exotic-looking blue-and-green fabric into her hands.

'That'll look stunning with your hair,' she told her.

Sophie stared at it in dismay.

'What am I supposed to do with it?' she asked unenthusiastically.

'It's a batik-print sarong,' the woman explained helpfully. 'I'll show you how to tie it, if you like.'

Sophie eventually emerged reluctantly from the dressing-room.

'I feel half-naked in this thing,' she muttered to Mandy.

'You look fantastic,' Mandy assured her.

'It's all right for you, Mandy.'

Her friend looked great in one of Betty's lacy, cotton knit tops and a batik sarong worn as a skirt.

Sophie jumped nervously as the music pounded into life. The fashion show was under way.

'Come on, Mandy, we're on!'

A jumper-clad Mike Barratt had suddenly materialised, grabbing Mandy by the hand.

'Oh, well, here goes!' Mandy said excitedly, allowing Mike to lead her out on to the makeshift catwalk.

Turning round, Sophie realised that James had materialised beside her. Her heart contracted painfully. He was the last person she wanted to see right then, she thought miserably.

'Very nice,' he grunted mockingly, his dark eyes flickering over the length of her body. 'But aren't you slightly underdressed?'

Sophie flushed, clutching her arms tightly to her body.

'I'm not the only one,' she muttered, eyeing

him in return.

James looked disarmingly attractive in his own dark trousers together with one of Jean's brightly-coloured waistcoats. Someone— probably Jean herself—had clearly insisted that he wear the waistcoat with nothing underneath, so that his muscular upper arms were revealed, together with a glimpse of his tanned chest.

'You've obviously missed your vocation as a male supermodel,' Sophie added sarcastically.

No-one would have guessed from her tone the hurt she was feeling inside.

'I don't know why I ever agreed to do this!' James grimaced, clearly ill-at-ease. 'I hope Mike Barratt realises he owes me one.'

'What a handsome couple!'

Old Betty Johnson appeared behind them, clapping her hands together delightedly, clearly oblivious to the heavy atmosphere between them. At that moment a breathless, exhilarated Mandy returned from the catwalk with Mike in tow.

'Off you go, you two. Good luck!'

She gave them both a little push in the direction of the stage. As they emerged from behind the curtains, the catwalk looked a mile long. Sophie's scowl deepened, as she vowed to get her revenge on Mandy for this. If this was her idea of matchmaking . . .

'For goodness' sake, smile, can't you?' James muttered as they made their entrance, to a ripple of applause.

Sophie's cheeks were burning with embarrassment as the two of them made their way down the catwalk, to the backdrop of music pulsating from the loudspeakers. At last they reached the end of the catwalk where they paused while Jean's commentary came over the loudspeakers.

'Sophie looks stunning in an electric blue and emerald batik-print sarong by Artisans, while James looks effortlessly handsome in a handmade silk waistcoat by Chapman's of Ecclesdon.'

Sophie hardly heard Jean's commentary, however, for at some point, as they posed for the audience, James's arm had made its way casually around her waist. It was all part of the performance, Sophie reminded herself as she felt the blush creeping up her face, part of their act at looking like a normal couple.

She gazed out at the audience of townspeople and summer visitors, suddenly noticing her parents, who waved encouragingly at her. Then she noticed Chris Atkins sitting beside her father. His eyes were fixed on James and he had an expression of extreme discontentment on his face.

That evening, James Harrison felt like a bear with a sore head. Seeking solace, he had gone out to his workshop, but today, not even his beloved woodturning could take his mind off things. True, it had been a successful day, in financial terms at least. He had never dreamed the items he designed and made himself would prove to be so popular with the public, but in another sense, the day had been a disaster.

It had started promisingly enough, he thought as he set the lathe spinning. After that misunderstanding over Mandy, Sophie had seemed to be going out of her way to be pleasant to him. So why had he, like a fool, refused to swallow his pride and persisted in snubbing her attempts at friendship? Because of that slimy little toe-rag Atkins, that was why!

His fist clenched around his chisel and his mouth firmed into a thin, pensive line. There was something about that Chris Atkins he didn't like. The little creep was oozing with confidence, and clearly an expert in smoothtalking women, despite his tender years.

His thoughts left Atkins, returning to Sophie. He hadn't meant to put his arm round her on the catwalk, of course. It was just that, somehow, whenever they were together, he was unable to keep away from her. Suddenly, he knew he had to talk to her. Impulsively, James abandoned his work and went inside to the phone.

She answered on the first ring.

'Sophie?'

'What do you want?' she sounded surprised.

'Are you busy?'

'No, I was just going to have a bath.'

'Well, postpone it. I need to talk to you.'

He put down the phone and went to get the car from the garage. Perhaps they could at least be friends, he thought, as he took the road back into town. Then he frowned. So much for his plans. He had never gone grovelling to a woman before.

Sophie answered the front door. She had been surprised when the phone rang, and even more so to hear James Harrison's voice. Now here he was, standing on her doorstep. Her heart leaped treacherously, then plummeted just as rapidly. What did he want now? Hadn't he caused her enough heartache for one day?

She was wondering whether or not to slam the door in his face when he said, 'I expect you're wondering why I'm here.'

'Well, yes, I was, actually,' Sophie admitted, momentarily disarmed.

James grimaced, as if uncertain of how to continue.

'I—I wanted to apologise for the way I behaved today.'

'So you admit you behaved badly.'

'Look, can I come in?'

Grudgingly, Sophie showed him into the small drawing-room.

'Can I get you a drink?'

James shook his head.

'Look, Sophie, I'm sorry if I spoke out of

69

turn earlier today. I don't know what got into me. Your relationship with Atkins is no business of mine.'

'You had no right to insult Chris. He's never done anyone any harm. At least I always get on well with him.'

'Whereas the two of us always fight like cat and dog,' James finished bitterly.

'Well, what have you got against the poor man?' Sophie demanded.

'I don't know. I suppose it's because he's everything I'm not,' he muttered. 'Sometimes, I just want to wipe that suave, charming smile right off his face!'

Sophie raised her eyebrows, surprised at this outburst.

'I never thought of you as a jealous man!'

And yet, she had to admit, the realisation made some of her misery recede, to be replaced by a warm glow inside. The smile died from her face, however, as a new thought struck her.

'Is that why you decided to maul me on the catwalk today?' she asked frostily. 'To score points off Chris?'

'No. You wouldn't believe me if I told you the real reason.'

'Try me,' Sophie challenged.

'What if I said it was because I found you irresistible?' James said quietly.

'You're joking, aren't you?' she said indignantly. 'Amusing yourself at my expense?'

'I've never been more serious,' he replied softly.

Suddenly it seemed as if the room had shrunk, and they were sitting very close together on the sofa. She found herself wondering if he was going to kiss her, and hoping that he would!

'Why did you come here?' she asked him abruptly, shattering the moment. 'I'm sure it wasn't just to carry out a post-mortem on the day's events.'

James looked away.

'I wondered if I could offer you a lift to the protest tomorrow, by way of a truce?'

Sophie was unable to suppress her surprise, both at the offer and at the fact that James Harrison was holding out the olive branch.

'But I thought you were determined never to set foot on the heath again.'

'Let's just say that I'm willing to give it another try.'

'Well, I had been intending to go to the heath tomorrow.'

Sophie hesitated.

'The protest's still going on, then?'

'Of course!' Sophie replied indignantly. 'You didn't think we'd give up that easily, did you?'

He shrugged, remaining silent.

'Steve Collins and a few other die-hards have set up a camp there,' Sophie explained, 'and I had intended to go along and show my support.'

'Is that a "yes", then?'

Still Sophie hesitated. She wasn't convinced that James had had a change of heart, but she supposed she shouldn't deter him as he had shown willing. And besides, she was unable to deny the way her heart leaped at the thought of seeing James again.

'OK,' she said cautiously. 'I accept your offer.'

'Great. I'll pick you up at seven tomorrow morning.'

By the time James's estate car rolled up outside her flat the next day, Sophie was already having second thoughts. What, she couldn't help wondering, was he up to now?

'What's behind this sudden change of heart then?' Sophie asked James as she clipped on her seatbelt.

'What change of heart?' James asked, driving off. 'I always said there were drawbacks to the scheme, but I still think Ecclesdon could benefit if the building of the supermarket went ahead.'

So her suspicions were confirmed. After all Sophie's attempts at persuading him, he still stuck as stubbornly to his original opinions as ever!

'How can a town possibly benefit by the destruction of its countryside?' she asked pointedly.

'I've said many times before that I think

72

such a development will do wonders for the local economy.'

'Try telling that to the animals whose lives will be threatened by the destruction of their natural habitat!'

James kept his eyes ahead but the corners of his mouth curved in a smile.

'I think we've been down this road before,' he remarked wryly.

'You might think it's funny.' Sophie frowned indignantly. 'But to me, it's hardly a laughing matter!'

She turned to glare out of the window, fixing her gaze on the calming view of rolling green fields and, beyond that, the sparkling sea. She was unable to remain quiet for long, however. A minute or so later she turned back to James.

'You still haven't told me why you've decided to go along to the protest today.'

'I just like to keep an open mind, that's all.'

'I said before that I don't think there's much point protesting against something if your heart's not in it. I mean—'

She broke off suddenly, realising that James was not listening to her, but was frowning at the temperature gauge on the dashboard.

'This car's burning up,' he said abruptly. 'We'd better find somewhere to pull over, fast.'

James found a small side road and a few minutes later he had the bonnet up. Sophie got out and strolled round to the front of the car.

'It's gone seven.'

She glanced at her wristwatch, sighing.

'The bulldozers are probably arriving at the heath by now.'

James did not even look up from his work.

'Have you got any idea what the problem is?' she asked, trying to remain patient.

'Fan belt's gone,' James muttered.

His hair was tousled and his face was already streaked with oil. Sophie had to fight the ludicrous temptation to smooth that streak of grease away. Instead she frowned. Despite owning a car herself, she knew little about how to fix one.

'Will it take long to put that right?'

'It should only take a few minutes, but it could be longer.'

'Longer?' Sophie echoed, aghast. 'By the time we get to the heath, it could all be over!'

'Well, perhaps you had better let me get back to my work, then,' James said, disappearing back under the bonnet.

For a few moments, Sophie stood and watched him work, but if there was one thing Sophie wasn't good at, it was standing by doing nothing. She felt powerless as she glanced at her watch, seeing the seconds tick by, while the sun rose steadily in the sky.

'It's typical that your car would break down, today of all days!' she muttered impatiently.

James raised his head from the bonnet again.

74

'Are you saying I sabotaged my car deliberately to stop you getting to the protest?'

'Of course not! But you must have known something like this would happen sooner or later.'

She flicked a scornful glance over the old car, exasperation making her irrational.

'Couldn't you have got yourself something a bit more reliable than this old banger?'

'Old banger?' James echoed, his eyes dark with anger. 'This car is a classic. I wouldn't dream of getting rid of it. And besides,' he added, turning away, 'it belonged to my father.'

Sophie bit her lip, her cheeks flushing shamefully. Trust her to go and put her foot in it! She went inside the car after that, letting James finish the repairs in silence.

After what seemed like hours but could only have been a matter of minutes, he slammed the bonnet shut and got back into the car. Sophie had never seen a look like that in his dark eyes before and, in spite of herself, she was nervous.

'James, I'm—I'm sorry about what I said earlier,' she offered timidly, in an attempt at making the peace. 'I don't know what got into me.'

James shook his head, staring straight ahead out of the windscreen.

'Think nothing of it. I'm over-sensitive about my father.'

Sophie had never heard James speaking so frankly about himself before and felt compelled to ask, 'Were the two of you very close?'

'We were generally a close-knit family, I suppose. And, yes, my father meant a lot to me.'

Sophie was silent, wondering at this new, softer side to James she had never dreamed existed.

'That was why I hated to see what happened to him.'

'What do you mean?'

'He had an office job in the city.' James sighed. 'Commuted in every day, year in, year out, for thirty years, all the time dreaming of the day he would retire.'

'And what happened?' Sophie asked, her voice hushed.

'A month before he was due to take early retirement, he had a heart attack and died.'

'I'm sorry,' she whispered, her heart going out to him.

James seemed so alone in his grief that suddenly Sophie found herself longing to put her arms round him and comfort him.

'I vowed I wouldn't end up like him,' James went on slowly, 'tied to a routine job for ever. I decided that life was too short.'

'Hence your dream of living in the countryside?' Sophie probed gently.

'I had to get away from the town. I wanted

to live in a beautiful place, doing a job I loved.'

Sophie nodded feelingly. That was why she had decided not to go to London in search of work, though she doubted her parents would ever understand that.

'Listen to me!' Suddenly James roused himself. 'I've been droning on about my own problems, boring you stupid!'

'Nonsense,' Sophie interrupted firmly. 'I wasn't bored at all. And besides, it has probably done you the world of good to get that off your chest.'

James nodded slowly.

'I've never talked to anyone about this before,' he admitted.

Sophie couldn't help feeling pleased. Did this perhaps mean he had forgiven her?

'We don't have to go to the heath today. We can go straight home if you prefer,' she suggested tentatively.

James shook his head.

'We're going to the protest, Sophie,' he said grimly, turning the keys in the ignition. 'I know how much this means to you.'

CHAPTER SIX

'That's strange.' James frowned as they neared the heath. 'There don't seem to be many cars parked here today.'

'Well,' Sophie said firmly, 'it's just as well we came, then.'

They had hardly set foot on the heath, however, when Steve Collins came loping towards them, his mobile phone clutched in one hand.

'Sophie!' he called. 'Where've you been? I've been trying to ring you all morning!'

As he reached them, Steve glanced at James with undisguised curiosity. Recognising the hint, Sophie made the introductions.

'James, this is Steve Collins, an old college friend of mine. Steve, this is James Harrison, who's just joined us at the craft shop. He's a carpenter,' she added, by way of explanation.

'Carpenter!' James interrupted, his tone gruffly indignant. 'I prefer to be called a woodturner,' he amended, glaring at Sophie.

Even in public they couldn't appear to be getting on together! The corners of Sophie's mouth curved in amusement. It was ridiculous the way they bickered over everything, even the smallest, most trifling details. Glancing across at James, she saw to her surprise that his dark eyes were twinkling, too. Steve's gaze flickered from one to the other of them, baffled by this private joke.

'Anyway,' Steve said briskly, getting back to business, 'the reason I was trying to ring you, Sophie, was to tell you not to bother coming up here today.'

'What?' Sophie asked, suddenly serious

once again.

'There's not much point in you being here today,' Steve repeated. 'You see, the council and the building contractors have agreed to hold a meeting with us tomorrow.'

'Steve, that's fantastic!' Sophie burst out, her eyes shining.

So all their efforts, all their months of campaigning had paid off. She glanced at James to share her joy, but his expression was dark and pensive, his emotions as usual unreadable.

Steve, however, grinned, nodding in agreement.

'So we've agreed to suspend all action in the meantime,' he explained, 'on the condition that the contractors suspend work on the heath. Of course, we're going to stay here in the meantime,' Steve added, gesturing towards the small encampment just visible on the edge of the forest. 'Just in case they decide to break their word. I'm sorry you two have had a wasted journey.'

At that moment, Steve's mobile phone shrilled.

'Excuse me,' he murmured, turning away.

'Nice bloke, that Steve Collins,' James commented when they were out of earshot, although his tone implied quite the opposite. 'Ex-boyfriend, is he?'

'No!' Sophie replied indignantly. 'Just because I'm friends with a man, it doesn't mean we have to be romantically involved with each other!'

James shook his head, clearly unconvinced.

'The way he was looking at you then, it was obvious he fancied you.'

Sophie's cheeks flamed furiously.

'Well, as far as I'm concerned, Steve Collins has always been just a friend.'

'Just a friend,' James echoed thoughtfully, nodding. 'You seem to have a lot of those, don't you?'

He didn't mention any names, but Sophie knew that they were both thinking of Chris Atkins. They both wondered if they were seeing things when, just at that moment, they saw none other than Chris Atkins, walking briskly down the hill towards them.

'Speak of the devil,' James muttered.

Sophie tried to look pleased to see him. After all, it was commendable of Chris to turn up. As manager of a supermarket, he must be a busy man, and at least he had dressed appropriately, she observed, his jeans and T-shirt smudged with dirt and his fair hair uncharacteristically tousled.

'Chris! So you decided to join us!' she greeted him, trying to inject some enthusiasm into her voice.

'Yes, I decided to give it a go.'

He turned his back on James, addressing himself exclusively to Sophie.

'But didn't they tell you it's all off for

today?'

Sophie nodded.

'Yes, it's fantastic news, isn't it?'

'I'll give you a lift home if you like,' Chris offered.

'Thanks, Chris, but I came here with James.'

'I'm sure your—er—friend wouldn't object if you decided to change your mind.'

'No, really, it's all right,' Sophie said firmly.

Chris opened his mouth to protest once more, to be abruptly silenced by James.

'Can't you see that Sophie has made her decision?' he said curtly.

For a moment, the two men confronted each other. Chris looked miserable, torn between standing up to James and the desire to escape.

'I'll see you, then, Sophie. 'Bye.'

When Chris had gone, Sophie turned to James.

'As I said before, I can stand up for myself, thank you.'

James nodded.

'I should know that by now. I honestly don't know what came over me just then.'

His eyes flickered in the direction of the retreating figure, and Sophie's mouth twisted. She knew very well what had come over him— Chris Atkins, to be precise.

'It was good of Chris to turn up,' she commented pointedly, to needle James, 'especially as I think he felt a bit out of place here.'

'He probably only came because he was hoping he might see you,' James muttered in reply, an annoying, knowing look in his eyes.

As they were walking back down the hill, Sophie stopped.

'Steve was right,' she said thoughtfully. 'I wouldn't trust those building contractors farther than I could throw them.'

She turned to James.

'You know, I think we should stay.'

'I really don't think that's necessary, Sophie.' James frowned. 'I'm sure the contractors intend to honour their word.'

'Well, you can go if you want to,' she said firmly, looking up at him, 'but I intend to stay.'

For a moment they faced each other, staring each other out.

'Well,' she asked impatiently, 'are you going?'

Somehow, Sophie sensed that the question held an underlying meaning. It was almost as if their very relationship hung on his decision.

'No,' James grunted eventually. 'I'll stay.'

And they strolled slowly back up the hill towards the encampment on the heath, the July sunshine warm on their backs.

*   *   *

'Mmm, I think I could stay here for ever.'

So far it had seemed more like a day's

holiday than anything else. Sophie and James had sat on the grass in the sun all morning while the heath remained quiet and there was no sign of the building contractors' vehicles. When lunchtime came, the handful of protestors from the camp invited them to share their meal.

'It certainly is beautiful here. I must admit, I'm beginning to see your point about saving this place.'

Suddenly he stopped, as if he had said too much. Changing the subject abruptly he asked, 'Shall we go for a walk?'

'OK.'

As Sophie got to her feet, it struck her that, for over three hours, they had managed to exist in each other's company without exchanging a cross word.

They made their way towards the scattering of trees on the edge of the heath, and, as if reading her mind, James murmured, 'You know, if our ceasefire continues much longer, we might be in danger of becoming friends.'

There was a hint of humour in his eyes, and Sophie had never noticed before the way they crinkled at the corners when he smiled. She smiled back at him. Somehow, the idea of having James as a friend seemed much less dangerous than any other possible relationship between them.

'And would that really be such a terrible thing?' she asked teasingly.

'I'm not like you, Sophie.' James shrugged. 'I'm quite a solitary person, I suppose. I suppose I've just always felt I work better on my own.'

Sophie's heart sank. It was almost as if he was warning her off.

'We're not so different,' she found herself telling him. 'I like my own company, too.'

They had reached a splendid oak tree that dominated the surrounding area, and Sophie laid her hand on its sturdy trunk.

'Being an only child, I spent much of my childhood alone,' she said, a wistful look entering her eyes. 'I used to roam the countryside all day in the holidays, picking flowers and climbing trees.'

James's voice cut into her thoughts.

'You were quite a tomboy, by the sound of it.' He smiled suddenly. 'I'll bet you're itching to climb this tree now.'

'No way! I bet I can't even remember how.'

Before she knew what was happening, James had placed his hands either side of her slender waist and lifted her effortlessly into the tree. For a moment his hands remained around her waist and their eyes, for once on a level, locked.

Sophie caught her breath. Suddenly she knew that she had been trying to deceive herself—she wanted much more than friendship from this man. When their lips met and they were kissing each other, hungrily, it

84

seemed the right thing, giving vent to all the pent-up passion and tension between them.

After a few moments, they pulled apart, Sophie's thoughts a whirl of confusion. Trying not to show her feelings, she avoided James's eyes, focusing her gaze on a point in the distance.

'There's a good view of the road from here,' she commented unsteadily, 'just in case the building contractors try any sneaky tricks!'

As soon as she had spoken, Sophie bit her lip, expecting a rebuke from James for slandering what he felt to be perfectly honourable men.

'Perhaps I'd better join you, then.'

He smiled, and within seconds, he had hoisted himself up into the tree beside Sophie.

'This takes me back a few years.'

Sophie grinned back at him, her spirits rallying.

'It's as if we're a couple of naughty schoolchildren, playing truant!'

Then his smile died and Sophie knew he was going to kiss her again. Instinctively she pulled away.

'What is it, Sophie?' he asked gently. 'Is it Atkins?'

Sophie shook her head.

'I don't intend getting involved with any man at the moment,' she told him, with a firmness she did not feel inside. 'For the time being, my work comes first.'

'How much do you make at the craft shop?' James asked.

'Enough to pay my bills,' Sophie retorted defensively—not that it was any business of his!

'And what do your parents think of your choice of career?' James continued to probe.

'I think they're coming round to the idea,' Sophie admitted. 'Slowly.'

'They weren't happy about it at first?' James pounced on the admission.

Sophie shook her head.

'They thought I could do better. They said what was the point of having a degree, if I didn't make use of it.'

'Did it ever occur to you that they might be right?'

'You told me yourself that you wanted to live in a beautiful place, doing a job you loved. Why is it so wrong for me to want the same?'

'You're right.'

James sighed, conceding defeat.

'As long as you're happy, that's the main thing.'

'Yes. I'm very happy with my life at the moment. I've got my work, my flat, my friends.'

She waved an arm at the landscape around her.

'And all this lovely countryside.'

'It's small wonder you haven't got room for a man in your life!' he remarked mockingly.

Desperate to change the subject away from herself, Sophie turned the tables on him.

'What about you? I bet you've had . . . relationships.' She paused delicately.

When he nodded slowly, Sophie flinched inwardly, although he was merely confirming what she had already known must be true.

'Nothing that lasted, though,' he said thoughtfully. 'I suppose I was the one to blame. I was always afraid of getting in too deep.'

'Is that another reason why you moved down here?' Sophie probed gently, afraid of what she would discover. 'To escape?'

'I suppose so. My life was too complicated. I wanted to simplify it, make a fresh start.'

James clamped his mouth abruptly shut then, as if he had revealed more about himself than he intended. The next moment, however, his whole body had gone tense and alert as he sniffed the air.

'I can smell smoke.'

He looked round, suddenly exclaiming, 'My God, the heath is on fire!'

Following the direction of his pointing finger, Sophie saw that he was right. The area of heath directly behind them was on fire, the crackling flames already reaching up towards the sky.

'We've got to get out of here, fast,' James muttered grimly.

He leaped down quickly from the tree—too

quickly, it seemed, for he missed his landing and gasped with pain, clutching his ankle.

'What is it, James, darling?'

Sophie scrambled to the ground, kneeling anxiously over him.

'Is your ankle broken?'

Somehow the word of endearment had slipped out, but it went unnoticed in the panic.

'Not broken, I don't think.'

James answered through gritted teeth. 'Just twisted.'

Sophie glanced anxiously behind her at the leaping flames, and the plume of smoke rising into the blue afternoon sky. The hot summer had meant that the heath was as dry as tinder, crackling furiously as the fire consumed it.

'I think it's getting nearer,' she said urgently. 'Do you think you can walk?'

James shook his head.

'I'll only slow you down. You go, and fetch help.'

Sophie glanced behind her again, her eyes doubtful. She licked her index finger, holding it in the air.

'The wind's blowing this way! That means the fire's coming towards us, and the camp!'

'For goodness' sake go, and get help!'

James's brown eyes were imploring. Something in them told Sophie that his anxiety was not for himself, but that she should get herself to safety. Sophie realised then that she would never desert him, for the simple reason that she had fallen in love with him!

'I'm not leaving you here,' she told him, surprised at how steady her voice sounded. 'Now you're going to try and get to your feet, and we'll see if you can walk.'

Acrid black smoke was everywhere, making Sophie choke on her words, her eyes smarting painfully. James stared at her defiantly, as if he was going to refuse to do as she told him. For a moment it was as if time stood still, all life suspended. Even the roar of the fire behind them seemed to be subdued.

Then, reluctantly, James staggered to his feet, leaning on Sophie for support as she slid her arm around his waist. Even in the circumstances, the close physical contact made her heart miss a beat.

'This is ridiculous! We'll never make it at this rate,' James muttered brusquely.

'Be quiet, will you?' Sophie scolded him. 'You need to concentrate all your effort on walking.'

James scowled at her but obediently fell silent. He did not complain aloud but Sophie could see him wincing every time he put his weight on his bad ankle. She was sure he had broken, rather than just twisted it. But somehow they made slow, painful progress down the hill, the heat of the fire like an enemy in pursuit behind them.

As they neared the now-abandoned camp, Steve Collins came running towards them.

'Sophie, James! Thank heavens you're safe!' he gasped, wafting away the choking black smoke. 'We've been looking everywhere for you!'

'Steve,' Sophie said breathlessly, 'help us, can you? I think James might have broken his ankle. He can't put any weight on it.'

'Stop fussing will you, woman? It's only a sprain,' James muttered.

Between them, Sophie and Steve helped James over the last few hundred yards or so to the roadside, where the other protestors were gathered.

'Are all the protestors from the camp accounted for?' James asked tersely as he hobbled along.

'Yes, thank goodness.' Steve nodded.

At that moment, the sound of wailing sirens broke into the sultry, summer air.

'The fire brigade,' Sophie murmured, weak with relief. 'And the police, too, by the look of it.'

'Someone phoned an ambulance, too,' Steve said. 'It should be here any minute.'

A young policeman was the first to get to them, an opened notebook already in his hand.

'Does any of you have any idea how the fire started?' he asked, after taking down their names and addresses.

'None whatsoever,' Steve answered firmly, taking charge. 'The fire started some distance from the camp, so it's highly unlikely that any of our protestors was responsible.'

'What about you two?' the young constable asked, turning to Sophie and James. 'Where were you when the fire broke out?'

'What?' Sophie asked absently, wondering when the ambulance would arrive. 'Oh, we were in the trees, to the north of the camp.'

'So the two of you had strayed some distance from the camp at around the time the fire started?' the policeman probed.

Sophie had been more intent on getting James some medical assistance than paying attention to the question. Suddenly, however, her attention snapped back to the policeman.

'Are you implying that we deliberately started the fire?' she asked indignantly.

She indicated James, pale and drawn beside her.

'Can't you see that this man is injured?'

'I wasn't implying anything, Miss Taylor,' the policeman interjected calmly. 'I was just wondering if it was possible that the fire could have been started accidentally.'

'Now look here,' James interrupted, momentarily forgetting his pain, 'if you think we would have been stupid enough to put our lives at risk . . .'

At that moment, the wailing of sirens again split the air, as an ambulance rounded the corner of the road. The ambulance crew immediately took over, bearing James away on a stretcher.

'You two had better come along as well,' one of the crew members said to Sophie and Steve. 'You must have had quite a shock, and you've probably inhaled some smoke, too.'

Inside the speeding ambulance, Sophie gazed anxiously at James, her heart filling with a mixture of emotions. He lay on a stretcher, quiet now that he had been given a sedative. Sophie, too, was exhausted. What a day it had been! Her mind was still reeling with the impact of all that had happened.

'How do you think the fire started?' she whispered to Steve.

'It could have been local kids, I suppose.'

'So you're sure one of the protestors didn't start it, not even by accident?'

Steve shook his head.

'We were very careful. We deliberately never left our camp fires unattended, and anyway, the fire started some distance north of our camp.'

'I thought as much.' Sophie nodded. 'As if we would risk damaging the heath when we were going to such trouble to save it!'

'Try telling that to the police.' Steve frowned.

'What do you mean?' Sophie asked.

'I have the feeling, Sophie,' Steve replied, his expression grim, 'that the blame for starting this fire is going to be laid very firmly at our door.'

CHAPTER SEVEN

'Excuse me,' Sophie said, approaching the nurse in the corridor. 'I'm looking for a Mr James Harrison.'

'Ah, yes.'

The nurse nodded in recognition.

'Are you Mrs Harrison?'

'Er, no. Just a friend.'

'Doctor said that he's OK, to be discharged today,' the nurse told her. 'Mr Harrison has just asked me to order him a taxi but, of course, we'd rather somebody accompanied him home.'

Poised in the doorway of his room, Sophie's heart turned over at the sight of James. His slight hospital pallor and gauntness only served to make him look more darkly handsome than ever. And yet there was a vulnerability about him that Sophie had never seen before.

She had to restrain herself from rushing to him and gathering him into her arms.

'What are you doing here?'

James, sitting on the bed, frowned as Sophie entered the small, private room.

'I thought the nurse was ordering me a taxi,' he mumbled.

Sophie's heart sank at this ungracious reception. But James was a very private man,

93

she reminded herself, and it probably irked him beyond measure to be seen like this.

'I rang the hospital last night to find out how you were,' she explained gently, 'and they told me they'd had to set your ankle under general anaesthetic, as it was a bad break, but that you'd be ready for visitors by morning. Then I met the nurse just now, who told me you'd been discharged, so I offered to give you a lift home. I thought it was the least I could do.'

James's face seemed to soften marginally at her evident concern.

'I didn't mean to be rude,' he muttered. 'I was just surprised to see you, I suppose. Thank you,' he added, 'it's very kind of you to come and collect me.'

Sophie nodded in acknowledgement, although inside her, her heart was sinking. During the long night she had just spent analysing her newly-discovered feelings, she had built up her hopes that somehow James hadn't meant what he had said about just being friends. But now he was treating her as if she were some well-meaning maiden aunt.

*　　　*　　　*

'Is this it?' James asked later as they crossed the carpark towards her old Ford Fiesta.

'Yes. Why?' Sophie asked defensively. 'I know it's not much to look at, but I've grown very fond of it over the years.'

To her chagrin, there was a hint of amusement in James's eyes.

'Don't you think it was a bit rich of you to call my car an old banger!' he commented as Sophie helped him in.

She flushed at the memory of her faux-pas.

'At least mine won't break down,' she replied as she slid into the driver's seat. She patted the steering-wheel. 'I make sure it's regularly checked and serviced.'

'I suppose the local garage owner is a friend of yours, too?'

James raised his eyebrows sardonically. Sophie pretended to be shocked.

'Are you implying that I offer favours of a dubious nature?' she asked him. 'One more smart remark and you'll be walking home!'

But there was a sparkle in her eye that belied the sternness of her words. They seemed to be getting on well, she thought more hopefully. So far, so good.

'You know, I've been thinking,' James said suddenly, when they were on their way home. 'Being in hospital gives you plenty of time for that.'

Sophie's heart leaped at his words. Could he mean that he had been thinking about his feelings for her?

'The fire,' James went on, shattering her hopes. 'You're not going to like this, Sophie, but I've a feeling that your Mr Atkins could be involved.'

'He's not my Mr Atkins! Chris is just a friend of my parents,' she said matter-of-factly.

Then she realised what James was implying. Momentarily she took her eyes off the road to glance at the man beside her.

'James, what are you saying?'

'I don't know,' James admitted, 'but what was he doing at the heath yesterday?'

'Chris was at the heath yesterday for the same reason as we were, to protest against the new supermarket.'

'Come off it, Sophie,' James said derisively. 'Chris Atkins doesn't care tuppence for Ecclesdon Heath. It was written all over his face yesterday morning. His heart just wasn't in it. You must see that, too.'

'I might say the same of you.'

Sophie raised her eyebrows.

'All that talk of keeping an open mind, when what you really mean is that you don't want to commit yourself either way.'

As she spoke it struck her that perhaps James was frightened of commitment—of any sort.

'Why do you think I bothered going yesterday, then?' he asked her.

'I've no idea.'

'Has it occurred to you,' James said quietly, 'that I went because of you?'

'Because of me?'

Sophie almost crashed the car into a ditch.

She swerved quickly.

'You went to the protest just to curry favour with me?'

'If you insist on putting it like that,' James muttered, 'yes.'

Sophie frowned as she manoeuvred the car round a bend in the road. Part of her was flattered by what James had said, while another part of her was filled with indignation.

'You're just as bad as me!' she exclaimed. 'You accused me of not really caring about the serious issues, but you're just the same!'

All the same, she couldn't deny her pleasure that her feelings meant so much to him. James ignored her comment.

'I don't know why,' he said frowning, 'but I'm sure Atkins is up to something.'

'James,' Sophie said very carefully and pointedly, 'I hope you realise you're accusing a long-standing friend of my family, without any real foundation whatsoever.'

Glancing across at James, Sophie saw his eyes darken.

'Perhaps you would be able to see the matter more clearly if you could keep your personal feelings out of it,' he said brusquely.

'Even if you had proof that Chris Atkins started the fire, what possible reason could he have for doing it?'

'I don't know,' James admitted. 'Forget I said anything.'

For a few minutes, they drove in silence,

Sophie fearing she had offended him yet again.

'This is it. Pull up here,' James said abruptly as they arrived at a picturesque cottage on the outskirts of Ecclesdon.

'What a pretty house!' Sophie couldn't help exclaiming, turning the engine off.

So this was his dream home in the country. It wasn't what she had expected at all. It was built of the soft grey stone that characterised the local buildings.

'It's even got roses growing around the door!' she added.

For a moment, Sophie wondered if James was really content living on his own, or if he dreamed of sharing his home with a woman he loved, and filling it with children. If so, Sophie envied the woman he eventually chose to help him fulfil his dream.

'Thank you for driving me home, Sophie,' James said, his polite tones cutting into her reveries.

'Don't mention it,' Sophie replied, equally polite.

'Damn!' James cursed under his breath the next moment as he tried to clamber out of the car unaided.

'Oh, let me!' Sophie sighed, getting out of the car and rushing round to his side.

He accepted her help but with as much bad a grace as ever. When Sophie moved to assist him down the path, however, he shrugged himself free of her grasp.

'I can manage by myself now, thank you, Sophie.'

'Do you have to be so independent all the time?' she asked him frustratedly. 'Can't you just accept some help for once in your life?'

'I'm sorry,' James muttered, and to her surprise, he did not say any more.

Inside, the cottage was simply but stylishly furnished, appealing to her artistic eye. Very much a bachelor pad, Sophie couldn't help thinking.

She had settled a reluctant James on the sofa and was about to offer to make some tea when she caught a glimpse of the view through the patio doors.

'What a gorgeous view of the hills!' she breathed, clasping her hands together in genuine delight. 'James, I hope you realise how lucky you are, waking up to that every day!'

'Of course, I do,' James admitted with a smile. 'It was that view that sold this house to me.'

Sophie's eyes dropped to take in James's neat, well-tended back garden. Towards the rear, half-hidden amongst the trees and bushes was a picturesque, wooden building, its exterior clad in halved tree-trunks.

'Is that your workshop?' she asked James over her shoulder. 'Did you build it yourself?'

Again James nodded. In spite of herself, Sophie was intrigued. She imagined the workshop to be the heart of this private lair James had constructed for himself, his inner sanctum. She turned back to him.

'Now,' she said firmly, 'you're going to tell me where your kitchen is, and I'm going to make us both a cup of tea.'

When she handed James a mug of tea a few minutes later, Sophie paused to study the group of photographs placed on the small table beside the sofa. She saw one of a middle-aged couple who were unmistakably James's parents, and felt a poignant stab of emotion at the sight of his father. When she noticed one of a delicately pretty, dark-haired young woman, she experienced a sharp pang of jealousy, then caught her breath in relief.

'Is that your sister?'

'Yes.' James gazed fondly at the picture. 'That's Susie.'

Sophie noticed again the tenderness in his voice when he spoke of his younger sister. Perhaps that explained his outdated attitude to women. He had been brought up to believe that women should be looked after, he had said. Suddenly Sophie found herself thinking that the idea of being looked after by James was not so bad after all.

'Have you been in touch with your family since your operation?' she asked James, handing him his tea.

'No, for the simple reason that there's no point worrying them unduly,' he replied.

'But surely they'd want to know,' Sophie persisted. 'After all, you're on your own down here.'

'Sophie, I am a grown man.'

James sighed exasperatedly.

'It's very kind of you to be concerned, but I don't need your pity or anyone else's,' he continued.

It's not pity, she wanted to tell him, it's love. But somehow the words stuck in her throat.

'If you're sure you're all right,' Sophie said hesitantly as their eyes met and she was vividly reminded of their passionate kiss on the heath.

'All I really want is some time on my own,' he muttered, looking away.

Suddenly Sophie realised.

'I'm sorry. I've been interfering,' she said, her heart sinking.

It wasn't like her to fuss, but then James seemed to bring out that side of her.

'I'll go now,' she murmured, not meeting his eyes.

*　　　*　　　*

Back home, Sophie had just managed to get working on some paintings to take with her to the shop the next day, when the doorbell rang. A plainclothes policeman and woman were standing on her doorstep, showing their identity cards.

'Miss Sophie Taylor?' the policeman asked.

'Yes,' Sophie replied shakily. 'Has someone had an accident?'

Her heart began to pound. Her first thoughts were for her parents, and James.

'No, we'd just like to ask you some questions, if that's all right.'

'Oh, yes,' Sophie replied, relieved. 'Do come inside.'

For the first time, the policeman looked awkward.

'Er, down at the station, if you don't mind.'

During the short journey to the police station, Sophie's mind was in a whirl. She was certain that this was to do with the fire, and had a horrible feeling that Steve's words had come true, and that the protesters would be made scapegoats for starting the fire.

She was being escorted to the reception desk when a voice said, 'Sophie!'

She glanced up, seeing the familiar tall, dark figure, also accompanied by two police officers.

'James!' she gasped, her voice echoing the surprise and suppressed outrage in his.

James turned to the policeman who was accompanying Sophie.

'Why have you arrested her?' he asked curtly. 'She's done nothing wrong.'

'We haven't arrested Miss Taylor,' the policeman explained patiently. 'We just want to ask her a few questions, that's all.'

James was no longer looking at the

policeman, but at Sophie. She met his gaze and their eyes locked for a couple of seconds, as if communicating all that was unsaid between them. Then, reluctantly, James allowed himself to be led away.

*   *   *

A couple of hours later, Sophie felt as if she couldn't answer one more question pertaining to the fire. They seemed to be going over the same ground again and again, and she had to make an effort to stay calm and not to allow the panic to rise within her.

Where was James now, she wondered anxiously. What was he doing? Was he all right?

Fortunately, at that moment, there was a knock on the door, and a policeman's head appeared round the door.

'Brian? Could you spare us a minute?'

To Sophie's relief, the interview was terminated.

'Can I get you some coffee?' the policewoman asked, and Sophie nodded gratefully.

She had hardly taken her first sip of it when the door of the small room opened again.

'All right, Miss Taylor,' Detective Inspector Williams said, 'you're free to go.'

'Why?' Sophie asked, startled. 'What's happened?'

'A man has just confessed to starting the fire.'

'What? Who?' Sophie was aghast, praying it wasn't James.

She remembered the intensity of the anger in his eyes. Surely he wouldn't lie to the police, just to protect her! The policeman's next words knocked her for six.

'A Mr Christopher Atkins,' he told her.

Sophie was speechless. She didn't know why, but in her mind's eye all she could see was Chris Atkins smiling as he once said to her, 'I'll warn you, Sophie, I never give up on something I want.'

CHAPTER EIGHT

The bell on the shop door jangled and Sophie jumped suddenly in surprise.

'Oh, hello, Tom. I wasn't expecting you for a few minutes yet.'

'Hello, Sophie,' the old man said gruffly, taking off his coat. 'Terrible business about the fire. It's good to see you back safe and sound.'

Sophie's mouth twisted wryly. News certainly travelled quickly in a small town. So far Mandy and her parents were the only people she had actually told of her ordeal.

'But of course,' Sophie said suddenly, remembering, 'your son's a policeman isn't he,

104

Tom?'

Tom's faded blue eyes gazed sympathetically at Sophie. His gruff voice softened slightly.

'You were friendly with Chris Atkins, weren't you?'

Sophie nodded dazedly.

'I still can't understand why Chris would do a thing like that.'

It was lunchtime, the shop was quiet, and after a moment's consideration Tom walked slowly over and turned the shop sign to CLOSED. He sat down on a stool beside Sophie.

'I shouldn't really be telling you this, but, well, it seems Chris Atkins was in line for the job of manager at the new supermarket.'

Somehow Sophie was not surprised. It all made so much sense. Chris was an ambitious, young man, and she recalled him saying that the out-of-town supermarkets were the way of the future. It was obvious he had had his heart set on the new manager's job.

'When it looked like the protestors were starting to win,' Tom went on, 'he was worried there might be no job after all.'

'But what good would setting fire to the heath do?'

Tom shrugged.

'It seems he thought the fire would be blamed on the protestors, and the council would refuse to continue negotiating with them.'

'And the building of the supermarket would go ahead,' Sophie added slowly.

'Exactly. Thank goodness he had an attack of conscience in the end, and decided to confess.'

Sophie nodded her agreement, a chill running down her spine.

'Goodness knows what would have happened to James and me if he hadn't.'

*   *   *

'You must come along to the meeting,' Steve Collins had told her. 'After all, you did play a crucial rôle in the battle for Ecclesdon Heath!'

As Sophie recalled Steve's dramatic words now, her mind went back to the drama and fraught emotion of the fire and its aftermath, and she shivered, despite the warm August sunshine. Would James be there today, she wondered. She hadn't seen him since that day at the police station.

It was now a fortnight later, and the meeting between the protestors, the council and the contractors had been rescheduled for today. Fortunately, because the fire brigade had arrived so promptly, the heath had survived the fire more or less unscathed. But they still had to save it from the building contractor's bulldozers.

She was crossing the grounds at the rear of

the town hall when a voice behind her made her jump.

'Sophie.'

Her heart lurched. James looked smarter than she had ever seen him, in a dark suit, even his normally tousled curls disciplined with gel. He looked slightly uncomfortable in his finery, as if he would rather be back amongst the dust and woodshavings of his workshop. The sight of him provoked a complicated mixture of emotions in her.

'James,' she said unsteadily. 'I wasn't sure if you would decide to turn up today.'

'Well,' he muttered drily, 'as you can see, here I am.'

He fell into stride beside her.

'Although to tell you the truth,' he went on, 'I don't know what I'm doing here. I can think of places I'd rather be on a morning like this.'

'How's your ankle?' Sophie asked, glancing down at it.

The plaster cast had gone, and the only trace of the injury was the fact that James hobbled slightly when he walked.

'I'm fine,' James replied briefly. 'What about you? I expect the last few days have been quite a strain for you.'

'What do you mean?' Sophie looked warily at him.

James paused tactfully for a moment, looking round to make sure they were alone.

'It can't have been very pleasant for you

when Atkins was arrested,' he said in a low voice.

Sophie bowed her head.

'No, it wasn't,' she said in a quiet, serious tone. 'My parents were very upset about it all,' she went on, her eyes darkening at the memory.

And she, Sophie added mentally, had realised she had never really known Chris Atkins at all. What would make a seemingly-normal, even respectable person do a thing like that?

It was small consolation to her to recall that Chris had believed she would not be staying at the heath on the day of the fire. He had still knowingly put the lives of innocent people at risk, all for the sake of his own personal ambition and greed.

'I know I had my suspicions about Atkins,' James admitted thoughtfully. 'But it still beats me why he did it.'

After a moment's hesitation, Sophie repeated what Tom Bradley had told her. While she was speaking, James's expression slowly changed from disbelief to anger.

When the meeting was over, Sophie fell into step with James as they descended the stone steps outside the town hall.

'You were supposed to be on our side!' Sophie hissed to James.

'This has never been about taking sides, Sophie,' James replied coolly.

It seemed nothing had changed between them.

'I noticed you soon forgot your reservations about attending the meeting,' Sophie remarked. 'I never knew you were such an eloquent public speaker.'

'And you responded by getting on your soapbox again, as your father might put it,' James replied.

Sophie scowled.

'Naturally I wanted to express my own views on the situation,' she said haughtily.

As soon as the meeting had got under way, their old arguments had sparked into life again, and for a moment Sophie had almost forgotten that she and James were not alone in that boardroom.

The council members had agreed with James that Ecclesdon was in dire need of decent, modern shopping facilities, and eventually a compromise was suggested, whereby the supermarket would be built on an area of scrubland to the east of Ecclesdon.

It was felt that as the supermarket would be farther out of town, there would be less of a threat to the local traders. They were going to apply for Ecclesdon Heath to be made a site of Special Scientific Interest.

'We got so far, only to back down at the last minute.'

Sophie sighed.

'I still can't believe that Steve agreed to the

compromise,' she added thoughtfully.

'Both sides agreed to the compromise,' James reminded her. 'If they hadn't, the stalemate would never have been broken. As it is, both sides are happy. The heath has been saved, and Ecclesdon will get its new supermarket.'

A voice in Sophie's head told her that James was right, that he had, in fact, been right all along in his insistence on keeping an open mind. She frowned. From the start, she had viewed him as her opponent, when perhaps he had never been her enemy at all.

'I suppose nothing in life is ever black and white,' she conceded grudgingly.

'What's this, Sophie? Surely you're not admitting defeat?'

He looked as though he did not altogether approve of the idea.

'Even when I agree with you I can't win!'

She turned to him provocatively.

'I suppose you're going to say now that you're disappointed in me, and that what you always admired about me was my spirit?'

'Something like that, yes.'

James smiled. They had reached the carpark.

'Can I give you a lift home?'

'I'd rather walk, thank you. It's not far,' Sophie replied.

James nodded.

'I know, you don't approve of using the car

for short journeys.'

Sophie also smiled.

'How did you guess?'

James's expression became serious. Sophie's heart leaped, sensing he was about to say something important.

'Sophie,' he began, 'I know we haven't always seen eye to eye, but—'

'Hey, you two! Wait for me!'

Sophie's heart sank as she turned round to see Steve Collins running towards them. Somehow, she sensed that she and James had missed their chance. It seemed they were destined never to be anything more than friends.

'Fantastic result,' Steve panted, catching up with them. 'Congratulations, you two.'

He turned to Sophie, a hint of apology in his eyes.

'I know they're still going ahead with the supermarket, but—'

Sophie shook her head.

'The main thing is that the heath has been saved,' she said firmly.

Steve nodded, turned to James, and shook his hand.

'Well done, mate. You were terrific in there. We'd never have got them to agree to the re-siting if it wasn't for you.'

James shook his head.

'It was a team effort,' he corrected, looking at both of them.

'I almost forgot,' Steve called as he was about to rush off. 'We're holding a party at the pavilion next Saturday to celebrate, and thank everyone for all their help. You two will be there, won't you?'

Sophie opened her mouth intending to decline politely. She had no desire to spend an evening in James's company, wondering about what might have been.

'Yes,' James answered for them both, surprising her. 'We'll be there.'

CHAPTER NINE

The next few days came and went in more of a state of normality. Sophie found her life was gradually getting back on track. Before she realised it, the day of the party had arrived.

For the umpteenth time, Sophie returned to the mirror. Everything was still immaculate— her hair, which she had put up into a chignon, her makeup, her olive-green dress that moulded itself softly to her figure and brought out the colour of her eyes. She glanced impatiently at her wristwatch. If James wasn't here soon, they would be late.

It wasn't far to the pavilion, but he had insisted on giving her a lift to the party. Yet with every passing minute, it began to seem more likely that he'd stood her up. Sophie glanced at her watch again. There were only a few minutes to go till the party began.

She snatched up her coat and stormed off. She might have known he would let her down, she fumed as she hurried along. Even as friends, their relationship was doomed. Oh, why hadn't she said she'd go in the taxi with Mandy and the others?

'Sophie! I thought you weren't coming! Are you all right?' Mandy said anxiously, on her arrival at the pavilion.

'I've just walked half a mile on two-inch heels,' Sophie muttered through clenched teeth. 'But apart from that, I'm fine!'

'Didn't James turn up?'

Sophie shook her head wordlessly, her green eyes suddenly brimming with tears. Mandy's face expressed all too clearly what she thought of James.

'Come on, Sophie,' she said. 'What you need is some of Jean's knockout punch. Then we'll go and find the others.'

Mandy was right. Sophie felt better after a few sips of Jean's heady brew. She glanced around her. The seafront pavilion was packed with townspeople, environmentalists and tradespeople alike. The others from the craft shop were gathered in one corner.

'Looks like the whole town's turned out tonight,' Jean remarked.

'Well, not quite all.'

Mary's hazel eyes narrowed meaningfully.

'There's one man from this town who won't be welcome here tonight,' she said.

They all knew whom she meant. Chris Atkins was currently on bail awaiting trial for arson.

'According to my son,' Tom said lowering his voice confidentially, 'they're running some psychiatric reports on Atkins at the moment.'

'Poor Chris.'

Sophie shook her head sadly, and everyone turned to look at her in surprise.

'I mean,' she went on, 'I can't help feeling sorry for him.'

'I can't say I agree with you,' Jean said, frowning.

Mary shook her head.

'That young man deserves to be locked up for what he did.'

Suddenly Mary's voice, even the rush of noise in the crowded hall, faded into silence. Sophie's eyes were rooted to the door, where James had just entered, followed by Mike Barrett, the silversmith. James looked devastatingly handsome in stone-coloured trousers and a dark jacket.

Sophie's mouth firmed grimly. No doubt those two had been at the pub having a pre-party drink, enjoying themselves so much that they had forgotten the time!

Sophie's frown deepened. She looked away in disgust.

Seconds later, she felt a hand on her arm.

'Sophie,' James said, his voice low and urgent. 'I need to speak to you, please.'

'Well, I've got nothing to say to you,' she muttered under her breath, snatching her arm away.

The next moment, however, James had seized her by the wrist and was dragging her firmly away through the crowd to a secluded corner.

'Hey, leave me alone!' she protested, but to no avail.

'Why did you run off like that?' James asked her in a low voice, when they were alone together. 'I was worried about you.'

'Worried?' Sophie rounded furiously on him.

'You've got a nerve, after standing me up like that'

To her chagrin he laughed.

'I had no intention of standing you up, Sophie. If you'd had a bit more patience and waited a few more minutes instead of rushing off, I could have driven you to the party as we arranged. But, no, time and Sophie Taylor wait for no man, or so it would seem to me.'

Sophie was angry at being laughed at.

'You still haven't apologised to me for being late!'

'I'm sorry, Sophie,' James said, suddenly serious. 'I tried to ring you to tell you I'd be a few minutes late, but you'd already gone.'

'Well, maybe if you hadn't spent so long in

the pub with Mike Barratt, you might have been on time.'

To her surprise, there was a tremor in Sophie's voice when she spoke.

'In the pub?' James echoed incredulously. 'I just gave Mike a lift to the party.'

'I see, so Mike comes before me, does he?'

Sophie was unpacified.

Suddenly, she realised that James had produced a miniature casket, which he was holding out to her.

'What's this?'

Puzzled, she took it, opening the lid. She gasped.

'That's one of Mike's rings!'

Mike Barratt's designs were unmistakable.

'It's—it's stunning!'

'No more so than you,' James said quietly.

Sophie gazed in silence at the perfect solitaire diamond, clasped in a delicately-crafted, golden band, nestling on a red velvet cushion.

'That's why I was late,' James explained in a low voice. 'Mike had only just finished working on the ring, and I was to be collecting it on my way over.'

Roughly, he grabbed her and, taking the ring out of its casket, he slid it on to her finger.

'Sophie, I can't wait any longer. I love you and I want you to marry me,' he said softly.

'Marry you?'

Sophie gazed confusedly up at him, thinking

back to that day at his cottage.

'But the other day you said you just wanted to be on your own.'

James grimaced.

'That was because I couldn't stand the thought of you feeling sorry for me. I didn't want your pity, Sophie, I wanted your love. I tried to convince myself we could be friends, but it's no good. It has to be all or nothing. Of course, I'll understand if your answer's no.'

'Yes.'

Sophie's eyes were brimming with tears again, but this time they were tears of happiness.

'What?'

'My answer's yes!' she repeated happily.

James's eyes narrowed warily.

'So Atkins means nothing to you?'

Sophie shook her head.

'He never meant anything to me. It's you I love, James.'

'Oh, Sophie.'

He took her roughly into his arms, kissing her with passionate intensity. After several seconds he let her go.

'I think I loved you ever since you smashed that damned jar of marmalade on the supermarket floor.'

'I smashed it?' Sophie echoed, pretending to be indignant. 'That jar would never have been broken if you hadn't been interfering in the first place.'

James growled exasperatedly, pulling her back into his arms. He was about to silence her with a kiss when Steve Collins appeared. It was the first time Sophie had ever seen Steve look embarrassed.

'Er, I'm sorry to interrupt, but could you two spare me a moment?'

James groaned, but Sophie would willingly have agreed to anything at that moment.

Smilingly she grabbed James by the hand, following Steve up on to the stage. Steve adjusted the microphone.

'Ladies and gentlemen, may I have your attention for one moment?'

The buzz of conversation around the room obediently diminished to silence. Sophie gazed down at a dazzling sea of faces, her colleagues and friends among them. She saw Mike Barratt with his arm draped casually around Mandy's shoulders, and was pleased for her friend.

'This party isn't about making speeches,' Steve began, 'it's to celebrate our achievement and to have fun.'

A cheer rose up from the crowd at his words.

'But we'd never have saved our heath, or our livelihoods, without your support, and particularly the support of these two, Sophie Taylor and James Harrison.'

He indicated Sophie and James, who looked embarrassed.

'They risked their lives to save Ecclesdon Heath.'

A huge cheer met his words, followed by a round of applause. Sophie felt James's arm slide around her waist, giving her strength.

'On a serious note,' Steve went on, 'your efforts will be appreciated by our children, grandchildren, and all future generations to come.'

At Steve's words, James squeezed Sophie tightly. Sophie knew he was thinking of the family they would have together, and she turned to gaze up at him, her eyes brimming with tears and her heart brimming with happiness.